PERIPHERAL VISION

The Black Coat Script Library

forthcoming

PERIPHERAL VISION

screenplay by
Andrew Paquette

A Black Coat Press Book

Acknowledgements: Thanks to my wife and daughter, who are very patient and kind, to Sean Reddick of William Morris who encouraged me to write, to my good friend Harry Kloor, who talked me into moving to Arizona and to David McDonnell for proofreading the typescript.

Visit our website at www.blackcoatpress.com

Introduction

This story started when I realized that I had only seen two supernatural thrillers that made any attempt to be consistent with the existing body of literature on the subject, *Ghost* and *The Exorcist*. For the most part, supernatural subjects are treated heavy-handedly; evil characters are one-dimensional and have no motive other than to destroy. Victims rarely have anything but redeeming qualities, and when it comes to their interactions with the supernatural, the focus is on the more sinister and terrifying aspects of the confrontation, ignoring a significant body of literature that describes a far more varied experience.

I actually did go to a street corner psychic as part of the research for the script. I wasn't expecting much, and didn't get much more than the authentic street corner psychic experience, but that's all I wanted. In *Peripheral Vision*, I tried to stay true to what my research described to me as components of an authentic supernatural experience of the possession type. I have not been completely faithful; though in spirit I believe I have conveyed the essential character of this syndrome of events.

The main character, Ethan Russell, is based on my father, who is a real boat pilot just like Ethan. Ethan is a lot like my dad, and I think that's why I enjoyed writing him so much. When I told my dad that I had written a script about a character who gets possessed, and he's the character, he enjoyed the irony. He also immediately wanted to check all the nautical details to make sure I got them right. After giving me a good talking to about why certain things were totally impossible, I promised to rewrite sections of the script to accommodate his knowledge of boats. In every case, it improved the script.

After finishing *Peripheral Vision*, I took a trip to New York City. While there, I dipped in on the Parapsychology Institute's reading room to check on a few things in the script.

It held up in the main, but I read about some very specific types of supernatural events I hadn't ever heard of before. Not only did I want to write about these subjects, but I also decided to put Ethan into a few more tricky positions. I hope my dad doesn't mind.

Andrew Paquette

Peripheral Vision

FADE IN:

<u>EXT. TRACK, SONOMA JUNIOR HIGH - DAY</u>
ETHAN RUSSELL jogs around a muddy track in rain and fog. Rain falls on him lightly, then heavier until it's raining buckets. Tattoos that were hidden by his dry T-shirt are exposed by soaking wet clothing. He runs powerfully but without interest.

Rain cascades into the track, falling heavily, obscuring everything.

<u>EXT. HOUSE - DAY</u>
A cloud of steam emerges from a vent beside the kitchen window. Rain splatters against the bare cement patio.

<u>INT. KITCHEN - DAY</u>
A bright-red shirt hangs on a spinner rack outside. It glows against steely grey rain and fog. Ethan now wears a spiffy white captain's uniform. He sips from a steaming cup of coffee as his laundry is drenched on the line outside. There is a plaintive meow from the sliding door.

A shivering, soaking wet cat rubs against the glass. Cat food floats in a plastic tray on the steps.

> ETHAN
> If you think you're getting in here like that, you're crazy.

He turns away from the miserable cat and opens the dishwasher. Outside, rain splatters against a nearby rooftop.

EXT. HOUSE - DAY

A Ford pickup is in the driveway. The garage door opens, re-vealing Ethan. Behind him, a weightlifting bench and a 500cc motorcycle. He turns to shut the door and the CAT darts in. He huddles in a corner, his yellow eyes glinting up at Ethan. Softening, Ethan pets the cat, who purrs loudly and rubs against his white uniform pants, smearing them with water, dirt and fur. He sneezes.

> ETHAN
>
> Lucky for you, ya don't haveta go work in this
> godawful mess.

EXT. GOLDEN GATE BRIDGE - NIGHT

Heavy rain splashes against mammoth red cables at the top of the bridge superstructure.

Dark rain clouds melt into each other in the distance.

Cars race by below, their lights blur into long ribbons of yellow and red in the glistening darkness. Lights from boats cross under the bridge.

EXT. FERRYBOAT - NIGHT

Rain smashes into the sides of a huge ferryboat. Through its many large square windows, wet commuters shiver against each other in the crowded interior. Outside, the boat deck benches sit empty and wet. The camera follows a short flight of steps to the wheelhouse.

EXT. WHEELHOUSE - NIGHT

Rain pours off the exterior parking controls. Ahead, a black, fog-enshrouded bay. A shadowy figure moves inside the wheelhouse: Ethan in his white uniform.

He drops the tiller inside the wheelhouse and approaches the joystick on the exterior controls. He manipulates them with confidence, smoothly maneuvering the boat's position into alignment with the dock.

EXT. SAUSALITO DOCK - NIGHT
The huge ferryboat approaches.

Deckhands throw thick yellow ropes to the dock where they are caught and quickly tied to pilings. Ethan walks back into the wheelhouse and out of sight.

The gangplank is slammed into position, allowing the commuters to exit. They walk quickly to get out of the rain.

INT. WHEELHOUSE, SHIFT ROOM - NIGHT
An overworked electric space heater mounted on the wall glows red in the semi-darkness. The room is tiny. It is decorated with miscellaneous boat paraphernalia, charts, textbooks, crosswords and a handful of "adult" magazines. SCOTT, a good-looking young man in a captain's uniform sits at a small desk studying a map of San Francisco Bay. The door behind him opens, revealing Ethan.

                    ETHAN
          Your turn, yuppie boy.

                    SCOTT
          How is it out there?

                    ETHAN
          Colder'n a witch's teat in a brass brassiere at the
          North Pole in the middle of an ice storm.

                    SCOTT
          That good, huh?

Ethan sneezes.

                    SCOTT (cont'd)
          You look like shit, Ethan. Are you all right?

Ethan does not look all right.

                    ETHAN
          I'm fine, you sissy teenager. In fact, I could eat a
          bucket of boogers right now.

                    SCOTT
          You should sleep this trip.

                    ETHAN
          Are you kiddin'? I'm gonna be too busy diggin' my
          filthy claws into the steel hull of this boat because
          I know it's being driven by a ten year-old who just
          got his license!

                    YOUNG CAPTAIN
                 (smiling)
          Thanks.

                    ETHAN
                 (genuine)
          You're OK in my book, Scott, even if you did just
          get your goddamned license.

Scott exits.

The bunks crammed in the back aren't all that comfortable,
but that's all there is. Someone's left one of those $25 X-rated
magazines on the lower bunk. Ethan looks at it with disgust
before stowing it in a cupboard.

EXT. OCEAN - NIGHT
Waves crest in small foaming whitecaps.

10

The ferry plows across the ocean.

INT. WHEELHOUSE - NIGHT
ETHAN sweats in his bunk, gasping for breath. He startles
awake, grabs the upper bunk.

The room rocks. Scott looks in from his seat at the controls.
Ethan closes his eyes again.

Scott puts some blankets on Ethan, exits.

Ethan throws up. He looks at the mess, gets out of the bunk.

INT. FERRY, RESTROOM - NIGHT
Harsh white light illuminates Ethan's face in the small metal
mirror. He slaps a steaming wet paper towel onto his forehead
and wipes his face with it. A twinge in his intestines. He is not
feeling good.

EXT. FERRYBOAT - NIGHT
Ethan carries a small stack of wet paper towels up the steps
towards the wheelhouse staircase. He's got to sneeze, but he
doesn't want to and he doesn't have a choice. When it happens, he reflexively covers his nose with the towels. He takes
the towels away, his face glows anemically in the rain.

INT. WHEELHOUSE - NIGHT
Scott looks up as Ethan enters.

                    ETHAN
                 (weakly)
         Hey, Scott, I got a test for ya!

                    SCOTT
         I'm afraid to ask.

ETHAN

It's a Rorschach test.

Ethan holds the soiled towel up for Scott to see. Scott is morti-
fied. Ethan is humored by his response.

ETHAN (cont'd)

I'm gonna go make some more.

Ethan returns to the shift room with purpose. Scott swallows
hard and turns his attention back to the boat.

EXT. SAUSALITO DOCK - NIGHT

Two short blasts from a foghorn, then the ferry appears from
within the rain. It sidles up to the dock.

The passenger ramp slams to the ground, allowing a sparse
group of passengers to disembark. Rain steams off the glass of
an outdoor light fixture.

Ethan and Scott exit the boat.

ETHAN

Thanks for taking over my shifts, Scott. You're a real
pal.

SCOTT

Always glad to help out a senior citizen.

ETHAN

Yeah, you punk.

Ethan grabs Scott in a headlock, Scott squirms.

SCOTT

Hey! Don't barf on me! I mean it!

                    ETHAN
     I'll barf on whomever I please my darling, now hold
     still, I can feel it coming...

Scott breaks free.

                    SCOTT
     Aaah!

                    ETHAN
     Good night, kid! Give my regards to Stef and the
     midgets.

EXT. PARKING LOT - NIGHT
Ethan walks across the lot to the Ford. He wipes his nose on a
paper towel before getting in. The engine roars to life, pump-
ing exhaust into the night air.

EXT. HIGHWAY - NIGHT
The truck lumbers around a dark curve.

The needle on Ethan's speedometer holds steady at 55.

Ethan looks out the windshield. His pallor is near white in the
glare of passing headlights.

Running lights on a tractor trailer glow in the rain. Ethan patiently slows down.

A motorcycle flashes by in the opposite direction.

Ethan is very ill. Beads of perspiration form on his face.

Traffic outside the truck literally moves in slow motion. Ethan
turns to watch a slow spray of water as a car passes. A bright
light crosses over his face.

THE SCREEN GOES WHITE.

Something flies out at us in slow motion, turning in the air as if weightless. It's a small photo on a chain. The face of a young girl smiles out at us from it. The chain crackles violently as it is pulled taught and snaps.

Then a chip of glass, and another, then several, and this is slow, so slow it's hard to tell what's really happening. A crack slowly grows out from the place the chips flew away from, more cracks.

The light is gone now and we can see again. We're looking at a piece of glass, and it's cracking all over the place. Hundreds of pieces of glass pull free and separate from the main mass, flying through the air.

A tree branch punches through the windshield, shattering it completely. Blood droplets smack into flying slivers of glass, rain pours in from outside. The landscape outside spins and now there's no more glass.

This is Ethan's POV as he flies through the windshield. A dark shape approaches and now we're moving fast. A load smack, a crash, a horn blaring, the truck rolling over an embankment, and...

FADE TO BLACK.

FADE IN:

Dark shapes swirl like smoke in a jar. Deep violets, dark reds, muddy oranges and blues dominate a spectral landscape of ghostly trees and highway. A glowing silver cord floats among the shapes, distant, stretching.

A car drives by, the driver's face illuminated by one of the Ford's red taillights. She is CONNIE WILCOX, a beautiful woman in her late thirties or early forties. A crucifix on her neck catches the light. A boy in the backseat (MATT) stares at the broken guardrail with fascination.

                    MATT
            (muted)
        Mom?

The woman reaches for her cell phone. The sound of her dialing mixes with the sound of an ambulance.

EXT. HIGHWAY - NIGHT
Telephone poles seen from above, white glowing raindrops plummet towards the upside-down truck.

Connie and her son stand to the side of a steep embankment with a great big chunk ripped out of the guardrail. Pan to the scene below.

The truck, upside-down on the hillside, wheels still spinning. EMS workers stand around the thing, getting Ethan into a stretcher.

EXT. HIGHWAY - NIGHT
An ambulance on a highway in the rain, white, soft, luminous. The image folds in on itself to reveal buildings, a street, a hospital.

EXT. HOSPITAL - NIGHT
Slow motion tracking of a covered stretcher to the entrance.

Close-up on a nameplate mounted just outside the emergency entrance. "Sonoma Memorial Hospital." Emergency red lights flash against the wall.

INT. O.R. SONOMA MEMORIAL HOSPITAL - NIGHT
Ethan rests on a table in the center of the room. He wears the clothes we saw earlier, but they are torn badly and bits of raw bloody flesh show through. Ethan shudders. Sweat drips down his forehead.

The O.R. doors are pushed open with a bang. Several DOCTORS and ATTENDANTS rush in to set up their machines.

An IV line is hooked into Ethan's arm. An Attendant picks glass out of Ethan's face.

> DOCTOR
> Katharine, would you please tell Mickey to get in here with the films?

> ATTENDANT
> They say it's going to be another five minutes...

> DOCTOR
> Right, then get me my smock. And a Tab, I'm bloody thirsty.

A THIN, GLOWING SILVER CORD dances in the air. It sticks up out of the space between Ethan's eyes and extends between the Doctor and the Attendant. It continues up towards the ceiling, floating unnoticed.

Crouched in a corner of the ceiling like *Spider-Man*, a semi-transparent ASTRAL ETHAN watches. His form is suffused with a dull brownish light. Closer examination reveals spines of light that protrude at right angles from his every surface. The colors are darkest in areas that correspond to the position of wounds on Ethan's body.

Below him, Katharine holds a smock while the Doctor gets into it. The view of Ethan on the table is blocked by men and machinery.

The Doctor sips from a cola can. "Tab" cola.

Astral Ethan fingers the silver cord. At first, he can rub it between his transparent fingers, but then it passes through them. He looks around.

The astral form of a TEN-YEAR-OLD GIRL (SHARI) floats near him. It's the girl from the photo in Ethan's truck.

                    ASTRAL SHARI
        Hello, Dad.

Astral Ethan blinks back surprise.

                    ASTRAL ETHAN
        Shari...?

                    ASTRAL SHARI
        I love you, Daddy.

Astral Ethan chokes on a welling up of emotion. As he does, the colors of his aura go dark, obliterating his view of Astral Shari.

                    ASTRAL ETHAN
        Shari? Come back...

INT. RECOVERY ROOM - DAWN
A pan of water rests on a stand near the window reflecting the dawn light from outside. Ripples extend outward from a dripping cloth as it is wrung by a NURSE.

Ethan rests in a nearby bed. Both of his legs are in casts, and bandages cover his chest. The nurse wipes his forehead with the cloth.

> ETHAN
> When...can I get...out of here?

The sound dims as they continue talking...

> NURSE
> If I knew that, I'd know a lot, now wouldn't I?

> ETHAN
> You should see me...when I'm not in bed...

The nurse straightens Ethan's sheets. Ethan catches her eye, then weakly flexes his biceps for her. He settles into his pillows with a smile as a faint hum becomes audible. The nurse continues with the sheets.

INT. RECOVERY ROOM - DAY

Rain pours down in buckets outside. Shadows from the rain drip down the walls inside.

Ethan sits propped up on his bed, completely absorbed by a soap opera on the ceiling-mounted television.

Connie, the beautiful driver we saw earlier, peeks in the open doorway. She has a wrapped gift under her arm (a book). She knocks.

> CONNIE
> Excuse me.

The soap opera is blaring on the TV. Ethan doesn't notice her.

                    CONNIE
          Are you Ethan Russell?

Ethan turns.

                    ETHAN
          Yeah?

He uses the remote to shut off the TV.

And there she is; modestly beautiful, dignified, feminine. She
is the spitting image of warmth personified.

                    CONNIE
          My name is Connie Wilcox, I phoned in your
          accident.

                    ETHAN
                (surprised)
          You did?

                    CONNIE
          Yes. I, I hope I'm not troubling you, Mr. Russell,
          I just wanted to see how you were doing. The wreck
          looked just terrible. I hate to think of anyone going
          through something like that.

                    ETHAN
          Well, jeez...

Ethan reaches over with his left hand to shake hers, but she's
just standing there.

Ethan is sitting with his hands to his sides. He hasn't moved.
Confused, he tries again and shakes her hand.

ETHAN
...it's nice to meet you, Connie.

CONNIE
I brought you something.

ETHAN
You gotta be kidding!

CONNIE
No. Here it is.

Connie hands him the package.

ETHAN
Jesus.

Ethan opens it. It's the latest collection of *New York Times* crosswords.

CONNIE
So that you don't get bored.

Ethan is stunned. A nice thing just happened to him.

CONNIE (cont'd)
I have to get back to work now. I just wanted to make sure you were all right. I hope you feel better.

ETHAN
I'll be fine.

CONNIE
I'm so sorry about what happened.

                    ETHAN
Why? I'm the stupid schmuck that went driving with
a 104 temperature.

                    CONNIE
Your family must be so worried.

                    ETHAN
They don't know about the wreck.

                    CONNIE
               (not understanding)
Oh?

                    ETHAN
I'm divorced. You're the first visitor I've had and
I don't even know you, ha!
               (he laughs, but it obviously hurts)
Hey, you gotta get back to work. Thanks fer droppin'
by.

                 CONNIE (cont'd)
...I can come back tomorrow, if you don't mind?

                    ETHAN
Look, really, it ain't necessary.

Connie is disappointed.

                    CONNIE
     OK.

Ethan is clearly uncomfortable.

                 CONNIE (cont'd)
     Are you in much pain?

ETHAN
Well it ain't exactly painless if ya don't mind my
sayin' so.

CONNIE
(brightly)
I'll go then, enjoy the crosswords.

ETHAN
Nice of you to drop by, Ms. Wilcox.

Ethan watches Connie leave. After she's gone, he pulls a
steaming blue plastic urinal out from under his blanket with
evident relief. Just then, the door opens again. It's Connie, and
she's smiling. Ethan hastily hides the urinal behind a lamp.

CONNIE (cont'd)
I forgot to give you this. My son made it for you.

Connie holds out a small envelope with "GET WELL SOON
MR. RUSSELL" scrawled across it. Inside, a figure made out
of Popsicle sticks glued together. The arms and legs are covered with drawings of bandages and casts. The eyes are a couple of 'X's" and the tongue is drawn sticking out.

Ethan can't keep a smile from crossing his face. Connie beams
as Ethan views her son's handiwork.

CONNIE (cont'd)
His name is Matt.

INT. RECOVERY ROOM - DAY
A NURSE makes the bed. Outside, radiant sunshine.

EXT. HOSPITAL GROUNDS - DAY
Ethan sits in a wheelchair across from Connie. He eats from a
nicely organized basket of food with gusto.

ETHAN

You really shouldn't keep coming out here.
I appreciate it, but you gotta have better things to do.

CONNIE
                    (genuine)
Not really.

ETHAN

Nice lady like you shouldn't be hangin' out with me.
I ain't got no manners and I'm a stupid lunk to boot.

CONNIE

I don't know anyone that's perfect, Ethan.

ETHAN

My ex would agree with you there, and she'd be
damn right.

CONNIE
                    (serious)
You shouldn't be so hard on yourself.

ETHAN

Tell it to my ex. If that poor lady hadn't met me, then
maybe she'd have better memories.

CONNIE

I seriously doubt you're so bad, nobody is.

ETHAN

Now don't get all mushy on me, it's too much fer my
delicate sensibilities.

Connie smiles.

                    ETHAN (cont'd)
          This chow is great by the way. You oughtta advertise
          or somethin'.

A hummingbird flits around a nearby flowering bush.

                    CONNIE
          Meet my little family and I'll cook a real dinner for
          you.

                    ETHAN
          You don't waste any time, do ya?

                    CONNIE
          There's no time to waste.

Ethan's heart pounds in his chest. Love beckons.

INT. HOSPITAL, HALLWAY - DAY
Connie wheels Ethan back to his room.

                    CONNIE
          Matt and I get along fine together. At first I didn't
          know what to do when Doak killed himself, but we
          moved up here from the city and we managed.

                    ETHAN
          I don't understand why any schmuck would do that
          with someone like you around.

                    CONNIE
          He had some things to work out.

                    ETHAN
          I'd like to work him out.

Connie messes up Ethan's hair.

ETHAN (cont'd)

Hey!

CONNIE

You men! Less bluster and more kindness, we'd all be better off.

ETHAN

Yeah, but we'd be less innaresting.

CONNIE

Is that what you think?

ETHAN

Nah.

CONNIE

You have to meet my son. You'd like him. You do like children, don't you?

ETHAN

Kids are great.

They continue down the hall in silence.

INT. RECOVERY ROOM - NIGHT

Moonlight shines in from outside, casting long shadows around the room. An audible hum increases in intensity as Ethan sleeps peacefully. He turns, and his body shimmers. The hum intensifies some more and now Ethan's body vibrates at the same frequency. He moves again and his body separates into two interpenetrating but independently mobile shapes. Restless, ASTRAL ETHAN moves beneath the sheets.

He stretches his arms and legs. Rubber-like, they extend to several feet beyond their natural length. In one movement, his limbs snap back to their right size and Astral Ethan tumbles upward into the air, upside down. Below him, his sleeping body bathed in moonlight.

A NURSE walks by outside in the hallway as Astral Ethan watches. Harsh fluorescent lights from above illuminate her face. Zoom in to the ceiling-mounted light fixture.

INT. APARTMENT - NIGHT

There's something wrong with the sound in this scene, it's muted and maybe the wrong speed, a bit fast, grainy even. Matt sits in front of a TV set doing his homework. He looks over his shoulder suddenly.

The front door opens and Connie enters with some groceries. The boy runs up to her to help with the bags.

                    CONNIE
          Matt! Not so fast!

                    MATT
          Sorry, Mom.

She kisses him on the forehead as he takes a bag.

                    CONNIE
          How was school today?

Astral Ethan watches from a corner, unnoticed by Connie or the boy. The colors of Astral Ethan's aura brighten a bit as he smiles. He follows Connie as she walks into another room. Her aura is faint, but pretty, all pinks and pale greens.

                    VOICE (V.O.)
                (dripping with malice)
          You are unprincipled. Worthless.

A blur of movement as an ASTRAL CREATURE slashes at Astral Ethan with ragged claws.

> VOICE (V.O., cont'd)
>
> Trash for trash.

A wave distortion pushes through the fine material of Astral Ethan's face. He is frightened.

Connie and Matt sort through the groceries, completely unconcerned and unaware.

> VOICE (V.O., cont'd)
>
> You will not harm them.

INT. RECOVERY ROOM - NIGHT
Ethan wakes, his heart beating loudly in his chest. Soft moonlight coats everything in his room with pale silvery highlights. Ethan waits for his heart to stop pounding, but it doesn't happen. With effort, he turns on a small table lamp and retrieves the crossword book Connie gave him. He flips through the pages and we see he's already completed many of the puzzles. He closes the book and lies back in the bed.

Above him, a swirling miasma of astral bodies swim against the ceiling.

> ETHAN
>
> Jesus.

In the center of these bodies, a staring figure. It's Ethan on his bed. We're looking down on the floor from above. Ethan shuts his eyes, the camera spins, and we

> FADE TO BLACK.

FADE IN:

INT. DOCTOR'S OFFICE - DAY

A Doctor unpacks an aircast from a box. It's the same guy that operated on Ethan before. Ethan watches as he rolls up his pant leg. Ethan can't keep his eyes off him.

                    DOCTOR
          You won't have to wear it long, just a few weeks.
          Your recovery's gone very well over all.

                    ETHAN
          Just so long as I can still fart...

                    DOCTOR
               (laughs)
          Of course.

                    ETHAN
               (serious)
          ...like a man.

                    DOCTOR
               (laughter)

Ethan grabs the straps on the cast and fastens them himself. He hops off the table, and crumples.

                    ETHAN
          Aagh!

The Doctor helps him up.

                    DOCTOR
          As I said, you'll need it for a few weeks. I'm thinking
          you might make good use of a pair of crutches too.
          Stay here.

ETHAN

I'll be fine.

Ethan turns to a pretty nurse walking by in the hallway.

ETHAN (cont'd)

I'm fine.

NURSE 2

I wouldn't know.

The Doctor returns with some crutches.

ETHAN

You mind if I ask you a question, doc?

DOCTOR

Shoot.

ETHAN

It's a really stupid question.

DOCTOR

Is there another kind?

ETHAN

I guess not. Look, when you were operating on me, were you drinking anything? You know, a soda? Like Tab or something?

DOCTOR
(shocked)
How in the world did you know that? You're supposed to be asleep!

ETHAN

I saw you. From above.

                    DOCTOR
          You did not! How could you?

                    ETHAN
          That's what I wanted to ask you.

The Doctor takes a dim view of the direction this conversation
is heading.

                    DOCTOR
          Nurse Grady said you were something of a practical
          joker, let's try those crutches, shall we?

EXT. DOCTOR'S OFFICE - DAY
Matt dashes up to the door and holds it open. Ethan exits the
building on crutches.

                    ETHAN
          Hey! Where's yer ma?

                    MATT
          In the car.

Connie waves from her tiny Honda Civic.

                    CONNIE
          Hey, big guy! Want a ride?

                    ETHAN
          Just so long as ya let me drive.

                    CONNIE
          No way, I know your record. Get in.

Matt holds the door open as Ethan climbs in the back. It's a
very small car.

                    ETHAN
        Too bad I ain't a dwarf.

Matt hands Ethan's crutches to him, making it even tighter.

INT. ETHAN'S HOUSE, KITCHEN - DAY
A bag full of groceries slams down on the kitchen table.
Connie immediately starts unpacking. Ethan watches glumly
from the living room, stranded on his crutches.

                    ETHAN
        Dont'cha need any help?

                    CONNIE
              (brightly)
        You rest, I've got everything under control here.

Matt enters, struggling with the weight of two grocery bags.
Ethan moves out of his way.

                    MATT
        Excuse me, Mr. Russell.

                    CONNIE
        You really should sit down, Ethan. Oh my goodness!

The inside of Ethan's refrigerator. Everything in it has either
liquefied or bloomed into a giant blue mold spore.

                    CONNIE (cont'd)
        Matty! Come help me baby, I'm going to need a
        bucket of water!

Ethan gives Matt a sympathetic look.

                    ETHAN
        You must have a clean house.

                      31

MATT

You got that right.

INT. ETHAN'S HOUSE, LIVING ROOM - NIGHT
Jay Leno on the TV, cutting up during his opening mono-
logue. Ethan sits in front of a tray laden with food as he
watches. It's funny, and he laughs. He reaches for a glass of
water, but his hand passes through it. He tries again, without
success.

ETHAN

What the hell?

Ethan bends down close to the glass and observes carefully as
his fingers penetrate it. Refocus to show a reflection of Ethan
from the wrong angle on the glass. Ethan spins, sees himself
sleeping on the couch. Astral Ethan gasps.

EXT. ASTRAL PLANE, TUNNEL
Astral Ethan falls down an endless vertical shaft at the center
of an infinitely long spiral stairwell. Iron bars grow out of the
banister and all the way up to the ceiling, making the staircase
resemble for all the world a prison cell block. Astral Ethan
continues to fall.

INT. ETHAN'S HOUSE, LIVING ROOM - NIGHT
Ethan starts awake. A late night erotic phone service ad greets
him from the TV.

TV

We have Swedish girls, Asian girls, Black girls and
dominant girls to fulfill your every desire. Call us
now, come be a part of our fantasy...

ETHAN
Shouldn't be sleeping on the damn couch.

He gets up, grabs his crutches, stumbles on the coffee table and spills his glass of water in the process. He shuts off the TV.

EXT. ETHAN'S HOUSE - DAY
A short street lined with identical houses. Outside of one, the cat stalks something in the bushes.

A lizard skitters around some large rocks near the door of the house. The cat paws at it.

Grunting from the open garage. Inside, a weightlifter's bench. Ethan sits under it in sweaty gym clothes while he presses a hefty looking set of weights on a barbell. He stops to wipe his face with a towel.

The cat looks in on Ethan, the lizard hanging from his mouth, its tail flopping listlessly. A phone rings, faint.

Ethan stands, winces.

INT. ETHAN'S HOUSE, KITCHEN - DAY
A door slams. Feet thump closer. Ethan lurches into the kitchen with a single crutch under his arm. He grabs the phone.

                    ETHAN
          Barkley? Whadaya want? It's Saturday!

INT. RED LINE, OFFICE - DAY
BARKLEY sits behind an incredibly messy desk. Outside, a ferry in its slip, the Golden Gate Bridge in the distance.

                    BARKLEY
          Ethan? How did you know it was me? Did the phone
          ring? I just dialed...

INT. ETHAN'S HOUSE, KITCHEN - DAY
Ethan wipes his face with the towel as he walks towards the refrigerator.

ETHAN
Of course it rang, why the hell do you think I picked up?

Ethan opens the refrigerator. Inside, a pie plate filled with gelatinous black muck. He pulls it from its shelf. Listening, he grabs a fork and heads over to the table.

ETHAN (cont'd)
Yeah, I can make it. I'll be in Sausalito at two. Yeah.

Ethan clicks the phone off and sets it on the table. He sticks the napkin in his shirt and has a bite of the goo.

Outside the window, Connie takes the laundry from the line. She looks in at Ethan, smiles broadly, waves.

Ethan drops his fork, grabs his crutch and hobbles to the door.

EXT. ETHAN'S HOUSE - DAY
Ethan emerges from the house, still wearing his napkin. The cat stalks him from the roof as he hobbles around the corner.

Ethan approaches CONNIE as she folds the last of the laundry into a basket. Above them both, the cat stares down at them.

CONNIE
Good morning, handsome.

ETHAN
You shouldn't be folding my laundry!

CONNIE
(brightly)
I don't mind. Anything for a friend.

ETHAN
But this is too much! You can't do everything for me.
I can take care of myself now. Besides, you got it all
wrong. Look at how you did the socks...

Ethan grabs a pair of socks and pulls them apart. He proceeds
to demonstrate how to fold them.

ETHAN (cont'd)
This is how we did it in the Navy. See?

CONNIE
I can do it that way too, you just need to show me
how.

The cat paws the roof, watching Ethan and Connie below.

CONNIE (cont'd)
I could help you around the house you know, maybe
we could help each other out...

She is close, beautiful.

CONNIE (cont'd)
...we might be good company for each other.

Ethan reaches for the laundry basket.

The cat tenses, readying to pounce.

ETHAN
(aroused)
Maybe we would, yeah, I kin see that, sure...

Connie approaches Ethan for a kiss.

The cat jumps onto Ethan's shoulder, knocking him to the ground, then bolts into the field behind the house.

> CONNIE (cont'd)
> What was that?

> ETHAN
> A cat. My daughter's.

> CONNIE
> I didn't know you had children.

> ETHAN
> "Had" children.

The cat runs through the grassy field.

> CONNIE
> Your wife has custody?

> ETHAN
> I don't wanna talk about it.

Connie is suddenly uncomfortable. She's hit a nerve and knows it.

> CONNIE
> Would you like to go out tonight?

> ETHAN
> I'll take ya, but I ain't dancing.

A light wind pushes the clothespins on the line. In the field beyond, the cat chases yellowjackets.

ETHAN (cont'd)
I gotta get to work.

EXT. FERRYBOAT, SAN FRANCISCO DOCK - DAY
A pair of beautiful women wearing summer clothing on the
main deck. Other passengers mill around.

ZOOM IN on the women, their faces.

SCOTT (O.S.)
This girl is definitely the one for me. You should see
her, Ethan.

ETHAN (O.S.)
Stef is the girl fer you, squirt, and you better
remember that or I'm gonna haveta turn ya in.

INT. WHEELHOUSE - DAY
Ethan clumsily grabs the binoculars from Scott, knocking his
crutches over in the process. He trains the 'nocs out the window towards the main deck below.

SCOTT
You wouldn't.

ETHAN
Yeah, so maybe I wouldn't, but you better watch it.
Sometimes, I worry about ya. Stef's a fine woman
an' a good wife, you gotta be responsible.

SCOTT
What about you?

Ethan grins as he stares through the binoculars.

ETHAN

I ain't married an' I'm gonna go blind from sheer
horniness if I don't do something about it soon.

SCOTT

Oh, you'll go far with Connie.

ETHAN

Thanks.

Ethan reaches into a bag and pulls out the urinal from the hospital, flips the cap off and takes a drink.

Scott is aghast.

SCOTT

What is that?

A big smile from Ethan.

ETHAN (cont'd)

Damn hospital charged me 80 bucks for this port
a potty, no way I'm letting it go to waste. Coffee?

SCOTT

I see the accident hasn't changed you a bit.

ETHAN

Now that's where you're wrong, sonny boy.

Ethan pours coffee for Scott.

SCOTT

What do you mean?

ETHAN

Ya think I'm gonna tell you, you bastard?

                    SCOTT
I don't feel like playing this game right now.

                    ETHAN
What game?

                    SCOTT
You know, you say "I ain't gonna tell ya", then I say
"come on please", and you say "no". And then I
really beg you to tell me and you say "oh, all right"
and you spill it.

                    ETHAN
I ain't gonna tell ya.

                    SCOTT
Ethan!

                    ETHAN
I ain't. But I'll tell ya this much, things'r funner now.

Scott pours himself another cup of coffee.

                    SCOTT (cont'd)
You will tell me. You know that, don't you? You
won't be able to hold it in, I know you.

                    ETHAN
Maybe.

                    SCOTT
Hmf.

Scott drinks. Ethan laughs.

EXT. GOLDEN GATE BRIDGE - DAY
The ferry crosses beneath the bridge.

                       39

A TRAMP watches it from above. He spits into the Bay.

> TRAMP
>
> Stupid people.

Cars flash by him as he huddles beside a huge orange girder. Some of the cars have their lights on, and the sky gets dark.

EXT. ETHAN'S HOUSE - DUSK
The cat walks along the rain gutter on the roof. The street is quiet but for the sound of late afternoon insects.

INT. ETHAN'S HOUSE, LIVING ROOM - DUSK
Ethan lies on his couch with shades drawn and lights out. A low frequency hum matches a barely detectable vibration in his body. He stiffens as the vibration intensifies, then his astral body slowly frees itself and floats upwards.

Astral Ethan's eyes are open and alert. A thin silver cord connects to his physical head lying still on the couch.

The room is quiet. Dust dances in shafts of waning sunlight. Astral Ethan takes in his surroundings, bobbing like a cork in the air. He squints, concentrating...

The room shifts...

> MORPH TO:

EXT. ASTRAL PLANE
Unformed dark colors and movement. A current of life. We're past it in the blink of an eye.

> MORPH TO:

INT. CONVENIENCE STORE - DUSK
Scott flinches, looks around. Another customer looks at him from the other side of the store.

CLERK

$22.83.

Scott returns his attention to the counter, where the clerk is busy bagging a six pack of beer and some toilet paper. Scott pays for the items, then leaves.

Astral Ethan follows Scott.

EXT. SIDEWALK - DUSK
Scott looks behind himself as he walks, looks straight through Astral Ethan.

EXT. SCOTT'S HOUSE - DUSK
Scott turns a corner, approaches a house with a brand new family sedan in the driveway.

Scott walks by the car while he fumbles in his pockets.

A set of keys spill out and land in some bushes growing beside the house.

SCOTT

Crap.

Scott sets his bag down and picks up the keys.

Scott opens his front door just as a little boy runs at him.

KID

Daddy!

The boy launches himself at Scott, forcing him to catch the boy. They wrestle.

In the background, a click, then footsteps.

> STEPHANIE
> Scotty?

STEPHANIE, a pleasant-looking woman in jeans and a baggy shirt peers around a corner at a disheveled Scott.

> STEPHANIE (cont'd)
> It's Ethan.

She hands Scott a portable phone.

INT. ETHAN'S HOUSE - NIGHT
Ethan sits on the couch with his feet propped up on the table, he talks into a portable phone.

> ETHAN
> I always say "crap" when I drop my keys in the
> bushes after spending $22.83 on a six pack of beer
> and other stuff at Hank's. I bet you do too. Don'tcha?
> I bet you do!

INT. SCOTT'S HOUSE - NIGHT
Scott is annoyed.

> SCOTT
> Stephanie told you that.

Stephanie mimes the question "What?"

INT. ETHAN'S HOUSE - NIGHT
Ethan excitedly pulls his feet from the tabletop as he continues his phone conversation.

ETHAN
How? You just got in... I ain't shitting you, buddy,
I was there. This is what's different, boy! That
accident changed me!

INT. SCOTT'S HOUSE - NIGHT
Stephanie watches as Scott replaces the phone's handset in its
cradle.

STEPHANIE
Did he want to trade shifts?

SCOTT
One of his practical jokes.

INT. ETHAN'S HOUSE, LIVING ROOM - NIGHT
The room has an airy blueness to it.

Outside, a strip of bright yellow flypaper twists in a light
breeze. A fly tries to unstick itself.

Ethan chuckles as he puts the phone back in the kitchen. He
stops to look at the table and the smile leaves his face. The
small picture from the truck sits there now, encased in a plastic baggy with some loose glass from its broken frame.

Ethan wishes he could see her again, craves the sound of her
laughter, but she's gone. The house is empty; of light, sound,
people, character, life, even dirt. It is immaculate. But Ethan
has an idea.

INT. ETHAN'S HOUSE, BEDROOM - NIGHT
A powerful hum permeates the room. Ethan lies on a neat four
poster bed in his boxers and a tanktop. He clutches Shari's
photo in his right hand. Energy pulses through the room. A
sourceless illumination damps darker, then lighter, then much
darker, then lighter again. Another pulse reduces the visual

details of the room to black silhouettes highlighted by a sharp blue rim halo. A flash of fast moving deep blue light and the room is transmogrified into a liquid, churning environment.

                                        MORPH TO:

EXT. ASTRAL PLANE
The room is gone. A high frequency vibration moves up and down Ethan's body, creating ripples in his skin as waves of astral matter wash through him. Needles of light coruscate around the entire surface of his body.

In the space around him, deep red violet wavelengths of liquid light merge with muddy yellows and greens. A patch of blue brightens, then separates from the main mass. It drifts up-wards, vanishing as it goes.

Barely discernible shapes swim into and out of the pulsing mass of motion-filled light.

Astral Ethan lifts out of Ethan, trailing wisps of astral filament from his heels. Ethan fades into a dark fog and is enveloped entirely.

In the far distance, trees, rocks and telephone poles seen from the air.

Astral Ethan smiles.

                    ASTRAL ETHAN
              (fx modification of Ethan's voice)
        Superman...

                              MORPH/WIPE TO:

EXT. HIGHWAY - NIGHT
POV ASTRAL ETHAN.

An aerial view of the highway from the previous scene. Tree-tops approach, then disappear just inches below. Leaves sparkle in the moonlight. Astral Ethan turns his head to look at something.

A caterpillar on a leaf at the very top of a tall tree. All forward motion slows to a crawl.

Astral Ethan bobs in the air near the caterpillar, fascinated.

Astral Ethan tries to touch the insect with his fingers. Just before making contact, spines of pink and green light leap up from the caterpillar to touch the lights around Astral Ethan's fingers. The colors travel into Astral Ethan's aura, dimming quickly as they are assimilated into his murky browns.

Astral Ethan looks over his shoulder, sees a telephone pole jutting out above the treetops. He reaches for it, stretches his body.

Telephone wires pass by rapidly beneath the camera. Astral Ethan's hand descends into frame and touches a transformer in passing. A jolt of current along the wire and Astral Ethan's speed is multiplied a hundredfold.

Astral Ethan's surprised expression dissolves into a muck of blue speed distortions and the background whips by even more quickly.

His hand is solidly locked into the current from the wire. It slides at incredible speed.

Astral Ethan is sucked along, a helpless prisoner of the current. He grins with childlike exhilaration.

He pulls at the hand as it races along, the fingers stretch, then separate from the thick cable.

A sudden cessation of forward motion and the background resolves itself into familiar shapes. The highway below reveals a single shambling Lincoln gracing its black curves.

Astral Ethan drops to the level of the Lincoln, pacing it.

Inside, an obese woman sits buried to her chest with car litter. A cigarette dangles from her lips.

> ASTRAL ETHAN
> My God, lady, you're gonna light yourself on fire!

The woman continues to watch the road, paying no heed to Astral Ethan. But then, Shari appears beside her. Shari looks straight at her father.

> SHARI
> You're in danger.

> ASTRAL ETHAN
> What do you mean?

> SHARI
> You're being followed.

Astral Ethan slows even more, allowing the car to continue without him.

The road pulses with the same effect seen earlier in his bedroom. With each pulse, the image disintegrates a little more, shadows crawling into corners, becoming other things. The music becomes sinister.

Astral Ethan turns his head as his forward speed diminishes to nothing. Something catches his eye...

A great, horrifying, slithering ASTRAL MONSTROSITY encumbered by thousands of hideous ASTRAL PARASITES.

A tremendous whooshing sound as Astral Ethan stretches into long ribbons of astral filament.

INT. ETHAN'S HOUSE, BEDROOM - NIGHT
Ethan sits stock upright in his bed, staring without seeing at his reflection in his dresser mirror.

SFX (heart pounding): Fwa-thump! Ka-Thump! Wham! Bam! Bam! Bam!

Ethan curls into his sheets, wrapping them tightly around his body. His heart continues pounding, unstoppable.

SFX (cont'd) (heart pounding): Bam! Bam! Bam! Bam!

EXT. ASTRAL PLANE
The Parasites astride the Monster. They wriggle and stare at us, completely devoid of intelligence. Their sleek fishlike muscularity undulates with horrifying power.

INT. ETHAN'S HOUSE, BEDROOM - NIGHT
CU Ethan's face, partially hidden behind a sheet held in a clenched fist, eyes tightly shut.

His room is ablaze with cool astral light, a slow motion liquid theatre of life. The doorbell rings faintly, then again, louder.

Ethan opens his eyes.

His room is back to normal.

EXT. ETHAN'S HOUSE - NIGHT
Ethan opens the door, revealing Connie, dressed for a night of dancing.

CONNIE
We've got all night, Matt's at a sleepover!

ETHAN
Gimme a second, I gotta change.

INT. CONNIE'S CAR - NIGHT
Wind tears through Ethan's hair. Connie drives. They are both relaxed. Ethan's crutches are crammed in the back.

EXT. GERMAN RESTAURANT - NIGHT
The car approaches a circular parking area in an elegantly decorated grove of trees. Pinpoint lights are strung around tree trunks like diamond necklaces. The handsome dark wood lodge shines with polish. A VALET runs up when they arrive.

Connie gets out, enchanted.

CONNIE
It's beautiful.

She hands over the keys.

CONNIE (cont'd)
Could you help my friend first? He'll need his crutches.

VALET
Yes, ma'am.

The valet runs around to the other side where Ethan reluctantly allows himself to be assisted. Connie smiles at him, the picture of innocence.

INT. GERMAN RESTAURANT - NIGHT
An oompah band in German folk costumes belt out a corny tune from the stage. Dancers fill the floor, happy, bubbling

with excitement. Ethan and Connie are shown to a private table.

                    CONNIE
        I'm glad you came out with me tonight, Ethan.

Connie twinkles in the candlelight, an apparition of honesty.

                    ETHAN
        Yeah, well, it's better than being stuck in traffic.

                    CONNIE
        I'd like to think it was because you wanted to be with
        me.

                    ETHAN
        The least I could do, a dinner out for all your help.

Connie reaches for Ethan's hand.

                    CONNIE
        You do...like me? Don't you, Ethan?

                    ETHAN
        Maybe I do. I just don't know where to go from here.
        I ain't exactly a saint, ya know.

                    CONNIE
        You're not so bad.

                    ETHAN
        Yeah, well, wait till you know me a little better.
        Besides, you need a husband, I just need a woman.

                    CONNIE
        I didn't think you were so cynical.

                    ETHAN
        I'm practical.

                    CONNIE
        I don't see how.

Connie pulls her hand from Ethan.

                    ETHAN
        Hey, Connie...

She dabs her eyes with a napkin.

                    ETHAN (cont'd)
        ...I like bein' with ya, don't get me wrong, but if we
        were together, it might be more responsibility than
        I could handle.

                    CONNIE
        It's better than nothing. I'm a lonely girl and I'm not
        getting any younger you know. I like you, Ethan.

                    ETHAN
        I...Connie, I just want to do the right thing by you.

                    CONNIE (cont'd)
        Don't worry about it! I haven't been with any man
        since Doak died. They all seem to get scared off and
        I'm left with bad memories. I need someone to love,
        and to love me.

EXT. ETHAN'S HOUSE - NIGHT
Moonlight casts twiggy shadows across the quiet street. A fine
dew coats Connie's car in the driveway.

INT. ETHAN'S HOUSE, BEDROOM - NIGHT
Connie's dress hangs neatly in the open closet alongside
Ethan's shirts.

Camera pans to the bed where Connie sleeps with Ethan. Her
arm drapes across his hairy tattooed chest.

The camera tilts up to take in the rest of the room. It is all silvery blue, clean, clear. Fine blobs of milky moonlight reflect
off polished wood furniture. The mirror, not a speck of dust on
it, reflects the quiet sleepers in bed.

Ethan gets up to look out the window.

A neighbor's messy yard. Plastic outdoor toys lay wet in the
dewy grass. He turns to Connie.

                    ETHAN
          Connie?

Ethan sits beside her, puts his hand on her shoulder.

                    ETHAN (cont'd)
          You think Matt likes boats?

INT. APARTMENT, HALLWAY - DAY
Ethan knocks on the door.

                    MATT (O.S.)
          Who is it?

                    ETHAN
          A crazy old sailor!

                    MATT (O.S.)
          Hello, Mr. Russell!

The door opens, revealing Matt, dressed in too many layers of clothing.

                    MATT (cont'd)
          Mom isn't ready yet.

                    ETHAN
          Jeez kid, yer gonna suffocate! You better take some
          of that off.

                    CONNIE (O.S.)
          It's cold out there! Don't listen to him, honey!

                    MATT
          Sorry, Mr. Russell.
                    (beat)
          I am hot.

                    ETHAN
          I'll bet.

Connie emerges, then locks the door.

                    CONNIE
          Everyone ready?

EXT. OCEAN - DAY
Beautiful sunshine, bright blue sky and waves. A small wooden sailboat slides by. Inside, Ethan, Connie and Matt. Matt mans the rudder with a huge grin on his face. Ethan sits beside him. All three wear new orange lifejackets. Ethan smiles openly for the first time.

The breeze catches Connie's wraparound skirt, exposing her shapely leg. She covers it quickly, but is happy to see that Ethan notices.

Sun glitters on the water.

Matt lies on the covered prow of the boat, using a crutch as a fishing pole.

Ethan and Connie sit together in the stern. Ethan puts his arm around her waist.

>   ETHAN
>   I do like you, Connie.

>   CONNIE
>   We like you too.

She turns and kisses him, deeply. Ethan caresses her.

>   VOICE (V.O.)
>   Unprincipled worthless scum.

Ethan pulls away from Connie.

>   VOICE (V.O., cont'd)
>   Murderer.

Ethan is frightened.

>   CONNIE
>   What is it? Is something wrong?

>   ETHAN
>   I'm going to check on Matt.

>   VOICE (V.O.)
>   Tread lightly, my friend.

A figure of an ASTRAL MAN forms in front of Ethan. He radiates hatred.

                    MATT
        Hey, Mr. Russell! Have you ever seen any dolphins
        out here?

The man disappears. Ethan is shaken.

                    MATT (cont'd)
        Mr. Russell?

                    ETHAN
        Yeah. Alla time.

EXT. OCEAN - DUSK
The sailboat cruises towards shore. A beautiful sunset casts
deep reds and oranges across everything in sight.

INT. DOCTOR'S OFFICE - DAY
CU nameplate on door: "Dr. Matthias Schnier."

INT. DR. SCHNIER'S OFFICE - DAY
Ethan sits shirtless on the examining table. The Doctor we saw
earlier removes a stethoscope.

                    ETHAN
        Scott's always tellin' me I'm sick, but he don't mean
        "sick," he means I'm sick, you know.

                    DOCTOR
        He is a boat pilot, I'm the doctor.

                    ETHAN
        I know, but...

                    DOCTOR
        You aren't ill, Ethan. You're in fine shape.

ETHAN

What about my head? Maybe I got a walkin'
concussion or something?

DOCTOR

(laughs)
I don't think so.

ETHAN

I saw this guy! He talked to me, scared the livin' crap
outta me!

DOCTOR

Why don't you give my friend Parker Caldwell a call,
he might be able to help you.

The Doctor writes some information down on a spare pre-
scription pad and hands it to Ethan.

ETHAN

He's a shrink, ain't he?

DOCTOR

A psychiatrist, yes.

EXT. MEDICAL BUILDING - DAY
Ethan exits the building. He crumples the phone number and
tosses it into a waste basket on the street corner.

Ethan continues down the street on foot.

EXT. GHIRARDELLI SQUARE, SAN FRANCISCO - DAY
Establishing shot on a nice day. Pan to a toy shop.

INT. TOY STORE - DAY
Racks of radio-controlled sailboats. A CLERK in his late fif-
ties wearing a workshop apron walks down an aisle with a

box. He sets it on a counter, where Ethan waits. He wears his aircasts, but doesn't have his crutches.

> CLERK
> One Billings Coast Guard cutter.

Ethan looks over the box.

> ETHAN
> This looks kinda babyish. Do ya have anything sleeker? A WSP10? A Flyvefisken?

> CLERK
> I've got the Flying Fish, but he's going to need help to build it.

> ETHAN
> Too complicated, huh?

> CLERK
> If he hasn't done it before, I should think so.

Ethan furrows his brow as if in thought, but then he puts his hand to his head and we see that he is in pain.

> CLERK (cont'd)
> Sir? Do you have a headache? Are you all right?

> ETHAN
> I'm fine.

> VOICE (V.O., whispered)
> You lie.

A black astral needle grows out of the space between Ethan's shoulder blades.

ETHAN (cont'd)

Eyagh!

Ethan grabs his back and slumps into the counter. He sweats, his face contorted in silent agony. Tears roll out of Ethan's eyes.

VOICE (V.O.)

(laughter)

More black needles appear in Ethan's back, pressing in. He whimpers in pain.

Ethan relaxes into the floor just as the clerk kneels down to help him.

CLERK

You're having a heart attack. I'm calling 911.

Ethan brushes him off.

ETHAN

Just gimme a second, I'll be...finengh!

Ethan takes a few breaths, one second he is in agony, the next...

CLERK

Better?

The needles dissolve into nothing.

ETHAN

(breathing deeply)

Peachy.

                    CLERK
        You should see a doctor. I had a heart attack four
        years ago. I didn't know what it was, but darned if it
        wasn't an attack. My wife made me go, saved my
        life.

Ethan gets up a little unsteadily.

The darker corners of the shop interior writhe with barely
visible astral forms. The clerk looks back at Ethan from the
middle of it, totally unaware of the activity around him.

                    ETHAN
        I ain't married.

EXT. STREET, SAN FRANCISCO - DAY
Ethan limps as he walks under an elevated section of freeway.
He carries a large package with the toy store logo under his
arm.

                    VOICE (V.O., quiet)
        Let's rest our feet for a bit.

Ethan turns to look and sees some homeless persons under a
bridge support. They ignore him.

Ahead, the Hyatt Regency Hotel.

                    VOICE (V.O., cont'd)
        That looks good. I've been there before.

EXT. HYATT PLAZA - DAY
Ethan crosses the crowded plaza. A beautiful woman passes
by, Ethan glances at her, continues towards the door.

                    VOICE (V.O.)
        We'll get her later.

Ethan shoves the door open forcefully.

INT. HYATT REGENCY ATRIUM - DAY
A beautiful fountain beneath a ten story glass ceiling. Glamor-
ous shops line the walls, well-dressed people populate the interior. A BOY and a GIRL sit beside their FATHER at a large
fountain, furtively snatching coins from the water.

Across the wide floor, a corridor with public phones and rest-
rooms. An elegant restaurant is situated among large potted
trees in the center. Ethan walks to the phones.

INT. HYATT REGENCY ATRIUM, PHONE ALCOVE -
DAY
Ethan holds the receiver in his hands as he tries to figure out
the instructions on his calling card. He starts to dial.

VOICE (V.O.)
Calling Connie? Trying to call Connie?

Ethan strikes the wrong number, has to hang up. He tries
again.

VOICE (V.O., cont'd)
How about someone new? Hang up, Ethan, you're
right, she's too good for you. You're bad.

ETHAN
(whispered)
This is crazy.

Ethan holds a torn-off piece of paper with Connie's number
written on it. He starts punching it in.

VOICE (V.O.)
6, 13, 42, 7...

Ethan hangs up and starts over.

>   VOICE (V.O., cont'd)
> 13, 20, 6, 6, 6...

Ethan hangs up again, chuckles uncomfortably. This is silly and he knows it. And again he dials the numbers, covering each number on the card with his thumb as he dials it. He gets to the last number...

>   VOICE (V.O., cont'd)
> Come on, let me dial. We'll get a slut, that's what
> you want, isn't it, Ethan? You said you'd go blind if
> you didn't, I heard you, I was there.

Ethan stabs the pound key. He slams the receiver onto its hook and spins around, trying to find the source of the voice.

>   ETHAN
> Would you shut up!

Some passersby overhear Ethan's outburst. They give him a disapproving look. Ethan is taken aback.

>   VOICE (V.O.)
> Let me dial.

>   ETHAN
> Goddamn hallucination. I just need some rest.

Ethan looks at his reflection in the polished chrome surfaces of the payphone. His face morphs to that of a JEERING MAN, the one he saw on the boat, then everything around him except for the telephone stall and the patch of linoleum it's attached to falls away from Ethan. In its place, Ethan stands stranded in the center of a whirling phantasmagoria from the astral plane. He falls onto the phone for support.

                    JEERING MAN
        You're half out already, why not go all the way?
        Let me deal with your problems, you don't like your
        life anyway. Think of Shari, you'll see her again,
        don't be selfish, Ethan, this is my body too...

Ethan clutches the phone booth unsteadily, gasping for breath.
Passersby ignore his disheveled condition. Ethan desperately
tears his plastic calling card to pieces as he mutters to himself.

                        ETHAN
        Shit. Shit. Goddamn it, what's happening?

                    JEERING MAN (V.O.)
        Let's get a drink.

INT/EXT. HYATT REGENCY ATRIUM, RESTAURANT -
DAY
Ethan sits at a café-style table furnished with a folding chair.
He stuffs his package under the table as a WAITER ap-
proaches.

                        WAITER
        Would you like to see our wine list?

                        ETHAN
        Just water, thanks.

                        WAITER
        Yes, sir.

                    JEERING MAN (V.O.)
        Whiskey would have been better.

                        ETHAN
        What?

                          WAITER
          Pardon?

                    JEERING MAN (V.O.)
          We want whiskey.

Ethan looks around. Most of the tables nearby are empty, but
one is occupied by TWO YOUNG WOMEN, probably college
students.

                    JEERING MAN (V.O., laughter)
          Whiskey is nice, but...

                          ETHAN
          ...wine is fine.

                          WAITER
          Red or white?

                    JEERING MAN (V.O.)
          Say white.

                          ETHAN
          White.

                    JEERING MAN (V.O.)
          (more laughter)

Ethan tries to disguise a smile on his face. He's confused. The
waiter leaves a menu on the table and walks away.

                    JEERING MAN (V.O.)
          Now raise our hand.

Ethan examines the menu.

                    JEERING MAN (V.O.)
          Raise your hand, Ethan.

Ethan taps the table with his fingers. The Jeering Man appears
sitting across from Ethan. Ethan is electrified by his presence.

                    JEERING MAN (cont'd)
          I know you resent Scott...

                         ETHAN
                    (whispered)
          Who are you?

                      JEERING MAN
          Who are you?

Ethan tries to surreptitiously look around to determine if anyone else sees his companion.

                      JEERING MAN
          Scott is constantly insulting you just because you
          didn't go to some fancy pants school. You went to
          'Nam and worked hard to stay alive while he was
          sucking on a baby bottle. He doesn't deserve to live.
          You should kill him.

The college girls stop their conversation to look at Ethan sitting alone at his table talking to himself.

                         ETHAN
                    (to himself)
          That's ridiculous.

                      JEERING MAN
          What about that hand, Ethan? Why don't you raise it
          now? Pretend we're in school and you have a
          question. Go on...

Ethan taps his hand against the table agitatedly. His face betrays a growing anger.

>   JEERING MAN
>   Raise our hand, Ethan! Do it!
>   (big)
>   *Now*!

INT. RESTAURANT, BAR - DAY
A BARTENDER nods her head towards one of the tables. The Waiter follows her glance.

>   BARTENDER
>   Looks like he wants something.

Ethan sits rigidly in his chair, holding his right hand high in the air.

The Waiter approaches Ethan.

>   WAITER
>   Are you ready to order?

Ethan stands.

>   ETHAN
>   I'm...sorry.

Ethan flattens the Waiter with a powerful punch to the head.

Ethan hobbles between the potted plants, leaving his package behind.

EXT. HYATT PLAZA - DAY
Ethan shoves his way through the revolving doors and hustles across the plaza.

EXT. STREET, SAN FRANCISCO - DAY

Ethan slows to a limping walk and self-consciously assumes a more "normal" pace. He sweats profusely.

> ETHAN
> I have to go back... Matt's boat...

> JEERING MAN (V.O.)
> No. It's my turn now.

Ethan's limp spontaneously disappears. He walks through the crowds, losing himself in them.

EXT. SLEAZY STREET, SAN FRANCISCO - NIGHT

Streetwalkers stand under streetlights at the corner. A new Ford truck is parked in an alley. The windows are all steamed up.

INT. TRUCK, ALLEY - NIGHT

A cheap PROSTITUTE with lipstick smeared across her cheek looks into the camera.

> PROSTITUTE
> Happy, lover?

She squats over a laconic Ethan who reclines across the bench seat. His shirt is open, exposing his lipstick-smeared chest.

> ETHAN
> Yeah.

> PROSTITUTE
> You ever get the itch, you know where to come, and come, and...

ETHAN
(scary)
Get out.

PROSTITUTE
Shit.

The prostitute hustles out of the truck, grabbing her clothes on the way.

Ethan looks in the mirror. He can see the prostitute struggling with her clothes outside. Refocus depth of field to see Ethan's face in the mirror.

ETHAN
You bastard.

JEERING MAN (V.O.)
I know, let's go tell Connie. She'll hate you and you'll never see her again.

Ethan's expression turns to stone.

ETHAN
You can go to hell.

JEERING MAN (V.O.)
Can I? Killer?

ETHAN
Stop calling me that.

JEERING MAN (V.O.)
Oh stop, you frighten me.

ETHAN
I am going to tell Connie.

                    JEERING MAN (V.O.)
You don't have the guts.

                    ETHAN
That's what you think.

Ethan slams into reverse, peeling rubber.

INT. CONNIE'S APARTMENT, KITCHEN - NIGHT
Ethan waits at the table as Connie pours some tea. She's
concerned.

                    ETHAN
          I'm sorry ta barge in on you like this Connie, I just
          wanted to see you.

                    CONNIE
That's all? There isn't anything else?

                    ETHAN
Isn't that what I said?

                    JEERING MAN (V.O.)
Coward. You won't tell her.

                    ETHAN
The hell I won't.

                    CONNIE
               (annoyed)
What did you say?

                    ETHAN
          Sorry, I'm talking to myself today...
               (nervous laughter)
          ...I was just sayin' uh, to myself that is, that I didn't
          have the guts to...

                        67

CONNIE

To what?

JEERING MAN (V.O.)

To what, Ethan? To tell her you just did it with a
whore? That you hear little voices in your head?
What?

ETHAN

...to tell you that I love you.

JEERING MAN (V.O.)

(laughter)

Connie is touched.

CONNIE

That's why you came all the way out here? Really?

ETHAN

(embarrassed)

Yeah.

CONNIE

Well, you're just full of surprises.

She kisses him.

JEERING MAN (V.O.)

That deserves a hug.

Ethan grabs Connie's hand, pulls her to him for a long hug. He
whispers into her ear...

ETHAN

Connie, I...

                    JEERING MAN (V.O.)
      Tell her. Or I will.

                         ETHAN
      ...I have to get back home.

Ethan breaks off and walks out. Connie is bewildered, not
knowing if she should be pleased or concerned.

INT. ETHAN'S HOUSE, BEDROOM - NIGHT
Ethan's clothes are strewn on the floor.

A weary Ethan stares into his mirror. Instead of his reflection,
the Jeering Man stares back at him.

                      JEERING MAN
      You are so much fun to play with, Ethan.

                         ETHAN
      Who the hell are you?

                      JEERING MAN
      You remind me of myself a little bit, except I don't
      remember who I am. Isn't that funny?

                         ETHAN
      A real hoot.

                      JEERING MAN
      All I know is, Connie. She's mine and no one can
      have her. No one!
                 (big)
      No one!

The Jeering Man morphs into a huge ASTRAL CREATURE,
the one we saw before. It leaps out of the mirror and slashes at

                           69

Ethan. It rakes Ethan again with huge claws, sending blood flying through the air.

> JEERING MAN/CREATURE
> (bellowing)
> Connie is mine!

Ethan tries in vain to escape, but the attempt is hopeless. The creature pins him to the bed and slashes him to bloody shreds.

Ethan lies on the bed, trying desperately to cling to his fast-fading life. The creature pauses his attack for a moment before playfully plucking at Ethan with a talon. Blood from Ethan's wounds flows freely into the sheets beneath him.

> ETHAN
> (very weak)
> ...why?

> JEERING MAN/CREATURE
> (louder than anything we've heard so far)
> BECAUSE...

Ethan's flesh bursts into flame, he screams...

> JEERING MAN/CREATURE
> ...IT'S FUN!

...and then, in a flash the flames disappear. One by one, Ethan's wounds seal themselves, his blood vanishes, and he's back to normal. The Jeering Man stands in front of him, laughing. Ethan's bed, his walls, everything is back to normal.

> JEERING MAN
> Really though, I want you to stay away from the lovely Mrs. Wilcox. Do that, and I'll leave you alone, really.

                         ETHAN
        I don't want to.

                      JEERING MAN
        OK, in that case, we'll be friends. That's fine with
        me. Hey, maybe I can help you with your grammar,
        who knows?

As he says this, the room stretches like taffy.

                                              MORPH TO:

EXT. ASTRAL PLANE
Astral Ethan opens his eyes.

                      JEERING MAN
        We can do a lot together.

MONSTERS swim through molten air towards Astral Ethan,
he screams.

INT. ETHAN'S HOUSE, BEDROOM - DAWN
Ethan sits up in bed. The clock on his dresser displays the
time: "5:18 A.M." He sits there, watching the clock, waiting
for the time to change, and it does, but slowly.

                         ETHAN
        This is so stupid.

Outside, first light casts long shadows across the street, shadows that stretch, and move, and separate from each other,
wriggling as if alive.
                                              MORPH TO:

EXT. ASTRAL PLANE
Connie approaches across a field writhing with snakes. As she
nears, her dress falls away to reveal extremely provocative

clothing. Her hair and makeup morph into a highly seductive style.

                    CONNIE
          Hello lover, want to kill me?

                    ASTRAL ETHAN
          I didn't kill her.

                    CONNIE
          It's OK, you can admit it.

                    ASTRAL ETHAN
          I didn't.

Connie slaps Astral Ethan across the face, slicing his cheek as if by razors.

                    CONNIE
          Don't lie to me! I can see your thoughts, your guilt!
          Tell me!

INT. ETHAN'S HOUSE, BEDROOM - DAWN
Ethan opens his eyes and rubs them.

                    ETHAN
          This is too much.

EXT. FIELD - DAWN
Dewdrops slide across leaves and drip off the ends. The cat shakes water out of its fur and trots to the fence which he jumps onto and then over to the other side. Ethan sits on the patio with a bowl of cat food between his legs. The cat circles Ethan, but won't get close enough to reach the food. Ethan is exhausted.

                              ETHAN
          Come on you dumb animal, what's the matter with
          ya?

The cat retreats to the bushes.

                         ETHAN (cont'd)
          Don'tcha like me anymore ya goddamn effeminate
          dog! Come on!

The cat just stares at him. Ethan gets up with resignation and
goes back into the house. When he's gone, the cat comes out
to eat from the bowl. Ethan watches from the other side of the
glass.

INT. ETHAN'S HOUSE, KITCHEN - DAWN
Ethan looks out the window at the cat.

                        JEERING MAN (V.O.)
          Let's sit in the middle of the floor.

                              ETHAN
          Screw you.

                        JEERING MAN (V.O.)
          Squat then. We'll rest a little. You're tired.

                              ETHAN
          I don't want to.

                        JEERING MAN (V.O.)
          Right there in the middle, go ahead. Get some rest.
          You need it.

                              ETHAN
          I don't like your idea of rest.

JEERING MAN (V.O.)
But it's comfortable there, you'll like it. Let's squat
on the floor, Ethan.

ETHAN
No.

JEERING MAN (V.O.)
You haven't had any sleep all night. Go on, rest.

Ethan shuffles to the middle of the floor and squats. His
tormentor laughs.

JEERING MAN (V.O.)
You are so weak! Look at you, just like a puppet!
(more laughter)
Pick your nose, Ethan! Pick it!

Ethan is enraged. He makes a fist.

The cat watches Ethan. Ethan is ashamed and infuriated.

ETHAN
No! No more! That's it!

He leaps to his feet, grabs a chair and hurls it across the room.

ETHAN (cont'd)
You hear me? Get out of my head!

Ethan grabs a microwave and slams it into the floor.

ETHAN (cont'd)
Out!

He throws a dish rack into a window.

ETHAN (cont'd)
Out!

He kicks cabinet doors in with his feet, slams his fists against every available surface.

ETHAN (cont'd)
Out of my head you miserable goddamned ghost!
Out! Out! Out!

He grabs the table and overturns it on the floor.

JEERING MAN (V.O.)
You are a funny man.

Ethan grabs his head between his hands and screams.

EXT. SONOMA GENERAL HOSPITAL, - DAY
Ethan's truck in the lot.

INT. EXAMINING ROOM - DAY
A WOMAN IN A DOCTOR'S JACKET enters carrying a clipboard. Ethan sits in his shorts on the table. Scars from the accident crisscross his many tattoos.

DOCTOR 2
The new scans are exactly the same as the ones we made when you were first admitted, completely normal. There are no undiscovered injuries in your brain, Mr. Russell.

ETHAN
I definitely know something's wrong, Doc. There is no way I'm in perfect health. None.

DOCTOR 2
Then help me out a little, why don't you tell me
what's going on?

ETHAN
Like I told Doc Schnier, I been havin' hallucinations.

DOCTOR 2
Auditory or visual?

ETHAN
(glum)
Both. They're real, like I could touch 'em. I never
thought hallucinations could be so real.

DOCTOR 2
What are you seeing?

ETHAN
Crazy stuff. Scary things.

DOCTOR 2
Are you suicidal or homicidal?

ETHAN
(beat)
I don't know.

INT. HOSPITAL, NURSES STATION - DAY
Connie leans over the counter as a NURSE punches keys on a
computer keyboard. She carries a basket of food with her.

CONNIE
Ethan Russell. They told me at his work he was
staying here. He's got to be here.

                    NURSE
          There we go, Russell, Ethan Edward. Room 1013.
          We got him all right.

                    CONNIE
          Thank you.

Connie starts to leave...

                    NURSE
          Hold up, honey, I have to let you in. He's in a locked
          ward.

INT. HOSPITAL, HALLWAY - DAY
Connie walks with the Nurse. She stops in front of a door and
nods her head towards it. Connie looks in through the window.

INT. HOSPITAL, ETHAN'S ROOM - DAY
Ethan reads a *Tom Clancy* novel.

The door opens and CONNIE enters.

                    CONNIE
          Hello, Ethan.

                    ETHAN
          Connie?

                    CONNIE
          I brought you some food...

She sets the basket near Ethan and gives him a kiss on his
forehead.

                    CONNIE (cont'd)
          What happened? The nurse wouldn't tell mc
          anything.

ETHAN

Amazing ain't it? She won't tell me anything either.

CONNIE
(not buying it)
Ethan! Does this have anything to do with last night?

ETHAN (cont'd)

OK, OK, I'll give it to ya straight. I got a brain tumor
and won't last more'n another six months. I, uh, I
didn't want anyone ta worry so I, uh...

CONNIE

Oh Ethan! If you don't want to tell me, well OK. I
just wanted to know. I do care about you, Ethan. You
worry me. A lot.

ETHAN
(grabbing her hand)
Hey, don't be mad. I'll call ya when I get out. OK?
They're just doin' some tests.

CONNIE

Will you be honest with me then?

ETHAN

No. I feel like enough of a freak as it is, wait until
I'm out. We'll have a good time then, but I still won't
tell ya.

Connie looks Ethan over.

CONNIE

You don't look sick. I don't see any injuries. You're
all there under the covers, aren't you?

78

ETHAN

Yeah, look, let's talk about something else.

CONNIE

Like what?

JEERING MAN (V.O.)

Let's talk about adultery.

The Jeering Man appears beside Connie.

ETHAN

About, about, adult, um...jeez Connie, these drugs...

CONNIE

Oh, stop playing with me.

JEERING MAN

I see your thoughts, why don't you tell her about
them? Tell her what you want from her.

ETHAN

Oh shi...Conn...Fu...I want to, ah. C-Connie, I want
to, man I can't do this...I can't be talking to you right
now.

CONNIE
(concerned)

You aren't joking, are you? Something's wrong isn't
it? Should I get a nurse?

JEERING MAN

Ask her about sex. See what she thinks.

ETHAN
(resisting the urge to do as suggested)

Nah, I'm fine.

                    JEERING MAN
Tell her to stay away.

                    ETHAN
I can't do that.

                    CONNIE
Can't do what?

                    ETHAN
Nothing. I'm just talking to myself here, to my
invisible friends...

                    CONNIE
Pardon?

                    JEERING MAN
Tell her to go. Tell her! Tell her to...

                    ETHAN
        (shouting as loud as he can)
...LEAVE!! Get away from me! Get out of here
before I kill you!

Connie bolts out of her seat in fear.

                    CONNIE
Ethan! What?

                    ETHAN
Nothing! I...

A ripple runs through Ethan. The Jeering Man's face flashes
across Ethan's face and is gone. Connie is shocked.

ETHAN (cont'd)
(whimpering)
...I don't know what's happening to me! Connie!

CONNIE
(trembling)
Pray with me, Ethan, pray for wisdom, for us.

INT. HOSPITAL, NURSES STATION - DAY
A loud crash from down the hall. A NURSE lazily looks up just in time to hear another crash. She rushes towards Ethan's room and flings the door wide, revealing Ethan standing on the bed, Connie kneeling on the floor, the basket of food strewn around, some of which is still sliding down the walls in a slippery mess.

NURSE
Mr. Russell!

INT. HOSPITAL, ETHAN'S ROOM - NIGHT
Ethan sleeps. Liquid drips from an IV and into his arm. A janitor scrubs food stains from the wall. Outside, leaves sparkle with fine dewdrops.

INT. HOSPITAL, ETHAN'S ROOM - DAY
Days of Our Lives on the ceiling-mounted television. Ethan sits up in bed and gives the program his full attention.

The female Doctor enters the room.

DOCTOR 2
Good morning, Ethan.

ETHAN
So far.

She takes his pulse as she talks.

DOCTOR 2

Have you had any hallucinations since the incident
with your friend?

ETHAN

What if I ain't?

DOCTOR 2
(smiling)
If you "ain't," then you won't mind if I kick you out?

ETHAN

Why the heck you wanna do somethin' as unladylike
as that?

DOCTOR 2

Your insurance company won't keep you here
indefinitely, and I can't think of a single valid
medical excuse for extending your stay.

ETHAN

But you know what happened! I don't want to hurt
anyone.

DOCTOR 2

You should have been on medication, we've
corrected that. You'll be fine now.

ETHAN

No offense, Doc, but that's bullshit.

DOCTOR 2

It's comforting to know how highly you regard my
professional medical opinion.

ETHAN

Sorry.

ETHAN (cont'd)
(beat)
Hey, look at my beautiful rugged smile.
(a manly smile)
What about that? You want me to stay, dontcha?

DOCTOR 2
No dice, sorry.

ETHAN
Have some heart for an old sailor.

DOCTOR 2
I'll make sure you get some complimentary Jell-O on
the way out.

ETHAN
That's going to solve everything.

DOCTOR 2
I'm sorry, Mr. Russell, I can't do any more.

ETHAN
(glum)
What if I paid for the room outta my own pocket?

DOCTOR 2
I'm sure it would be far too costly for you. I'm sorry.

ETHAN
I gotta go?

She nods. Ethan is simultaneously heartbroken and terrified.

EXT. OCEAN - DAY
San Francisco Bay glitters in brilliant sunshine.

The ferry approaches. On the outer decks, passengers wear warm clothing. Wind whips the flag flying from atop the wheelhouse.

INT. WHEELHOUSE - DAY
Ethan mans the rudder wearing a thick woolen sweater and sunglasses.

Through the window, deck two is visible. Commuters shiver from a piercing wind as the ferry's prow parts the waves.

Ethan sips from a coffee mug on the dash. He picks up the binoculars. Behind him, Scott enters from the break room.

> SCOTT
> Hey, Ethan. Want anything from the Greeks?

> ETHAN
> A million bucks.

> SCOTT
> No, no, no. I mean like coffee, donuts, baklava. That sort of thing.

> ETHAN
> They won't give me money? Well shit, I guess I'll have coffee and baklava then.

> SCOTT
> You worry me sometimes.

> ETHAN
> It's because I'm so manly.

> SCOTT
> That must be it. Hey, Ethan?

ETHAN

Yeah, Sparky?

SCOTT

How do you feel? I mean, you know... after the
hospital.

ETHAN

Like a boomerang. Bent. Get the coffee.

SCOTT

Back in a few.

Scott exits.

Sunlight glints off of Ethan's sunglasses. His face is expressionless.

A flash of light.

EXT. ASTRAL PLANE

An exact duplicate of the ferry, but this one is motionless.
Instead of water, an unending plane built of the swimming
bodies of small animal-like demons. Astral Ethan stands at the
rudder, bathed in light from outside. The Jeering Man stands
beside Astral Ethan, dressed in an identical captain's uniform.
All is cold and quiet. Motion is quick, but hidden just at the
edges of the camera's periphery.

JEERING MAN

You tried to thwart me. You won't do it again.

ASTRAL ETHAN

I will.

JEERING MAN

I will destroy you first. You, and all you hold dear.

85

ASTRAL ETHAN

Try it.

INT. FERRY, CONCESSION - DAY

Scott chats up a pretty PASSENGER while he pays for a small tray of food and drinks. He looks up at the clock nervously.

PASSENGER

I thought you captains were supposed to drive the ship?

SCOTT

This boat is loaded with pilots. It's not my shift.

PASSENGER

So you don't have to work right now?

SCOTT

Not exactly, I...

The boat shudders.

SCOTT (cont'd)

What? Christ!

The entire boat tilts radically and goes into a tight turn. Everything and everyone that isn't bolted down slides across the floor. Scott scrambles to the exit and runs outside.

EXT. FERRYBOAT - DAY

The boat tilts at a dangerously steep angle while turning. Scott races up the wheelhouse steps.

SCOTT (cont'd)

Ethan!

INT. WHEELHOUSE - DAY

Ethan grins malevolently as he grinds his chest into the throttle and holds the rudder fast. The boat spins in a circle.

                    SCOTT
          Let go of the rudder!

                    ETHAN
          Make me.

Scott rushes him, but Ethan resists. They fight for control of the boat. Ethan claws Scott's face, scratching him deeply. Ethan gets a stranglehold on Scott with one hand and squeezes with inhuman strength. Scott's face changes color to a bluish hue.

A heavy hand brings a pair of binoculars crashing down on Ethan's head, once, twice, three times and Ethan releases Scott. Two deckhands tackle Ethan and it takes all their strength to wrestle him to the ground.

                    ETHAN (cont'd)
          Didn't know this was a merry-go-round, did ya,
          Scott? Did ya? (laughter)

Scott gets to his feet with the help of one of the deckhands.

                    SCOTT
               (rasping)
          Gus, I...

He points to the clearly defined impressions left by Ethan's fingers on his throat.

                    SCOTT (cont'd)
               (rasping)
          ...get him below.

                              GUS
          You got it.

Scott brings the boat back under control. The deckhands haul
Ethan outside.

<u>INT. RED LINE, OFFICE - DAY</u>
Ethan sits stiffly on a chair facing Barkley's empty desk. A fat
bandage decorates his scalp where he was hit by the binocs.
Outside, the ferry leaves the pier. Barkley stomps into the office and sits behind his desk.

                           BARKLEY
          I'm so pissed off right now I can't even talk.

                            ETHAN
                          (pleading)
          David...

                           BARKLEY
          I am homicidally angry. Do you know what I mean?
          We have over 300 complaints because of that stunt
          you pulled today. Three hundred! I thought you were
          sober these days, you moron!

                            ETHAN
          I wasn't drunk, I blacked out, I don't know what
          happened.

                           BARKLEY
          You stupid shit for brains asshole! I don't care why it
          happened, it happened and that's enough.

                            ETHAN
          Ya ain't gonna fire me, are ya, Dave?

BARKLEY
What do you think? The Coast Guard pulled your
license, how the hell are you supposed to pilot a
boat? Yes, you're fired. Your medical benefits run
out in 30 days, I suggest you use them while you can.

Ethan gets up to leave. He holds his hand out for Barkley to
shake.

BARKLEY (cont'd)
Not on your life.

EXT. RED LINE, WHARF - DAY
Ethan stands outside the building, waiting in the parking area.

JEERING MAN (V.O.)
It was fun manipulating your body. Maybe you don't
have to stay away from Connie after all...

ETHAN
What are you saying?

JEERING MAN (V.O.)
You can be with her for awhile, and then you'll black
out and I'll take over for a few hours. That would
work nicely, what do you say?

ETHAN
Go screw yourself.

JEERING MAN (V.O.)
I don't think I like your attitude.

ETHAN
Yeah, so what?

Ethan kicks a rock. He rubs his hands together, they're shaking, badly.

A yellow cab drives up and honks.

INT. CAB, IN TRAFFIC - DAY
Ethan is nervous. The foreign CABBIE looks at him in the rearview mirror as they approach the Golden Gate Bridge.

> CABBIE
> You must pay extra for the toll.

> ETHAN
> There's no charge to leave the city.

> CABBIE
> But I must return. You will have to pay it.

Ethan's hands shake uncontrollably. He tries to disguise their movement.

> ETHAN
> Yeah, OK. Whatever.

> JEERING MAN (V.O.)
> Kill him.

Ethan wipes some sweat from his forehead with a very shaky hand. The Cabbie watches him from the rearview mirror.

The Jeering Man now sits beside Ethan.

> JEERING MAN
> He can get a fare on the way back. Why should you pay?

                    ETHAN
               (whispered)
          I'll let it go this time. He's OK.

                 JEERING MAN
          He is dishonest.

                    ETHAN
               (whispered)
          Don't, don't please don't make me do anything...

                 JEERING MAN
          You do what you like, you have free will.

                    ETHAN
          I don't want to do anything.

                 JEERING MAN
          Doesn't it bother you that he's going to sit there and
          grin while he takes your money? You've just lost
          your job and yet this man is going to help himself to
          what little you have left?

                    ETHAN
          I wish he wouldn't.

                 JEERING MAN
          But he will if you let him. You should punish him, set
          an example.

                    ETHAN
          I don't need to.

The Cabbie sees Ethan mumbling to himself. He slides his
hand under his seat and pulls a gun out, within easy reach.

                         JEERING MAN
          Kill him and get it over with. He'll die anyway and
          you want him dead now.

                            ETHAN
          No, I don't.

                         JEERING MAN
          Sure you do. Here, I'll help you out. Give me your
          hands... come on now, this will be easy, just like the
          boat...

EXT. HIGHWAY, THE RAINBOW TUNNEL - DAY
The cab drives into the tunnel.

INT. CAB, TUNNEL - DAY
Ethan leans forward in his seat.

The Cabbie slips his finger into the trigger guard of his hand-
gun.

Ethan wraps one arm around the Cabbie's neck while grabbing
the steering wheel with the other. He pulls hard, snapping the
man's neck like a toothpick.

A bullet shatters the windshield. The sound of another bullet
firing.

There is a screeching of brakes.

EXT. VINEYARD - DAY
The cab pulls in behind a stand of trees.

Ethan cuts the motor. To his side, the dead Cabbie lolls his
head with the motion of the car.

Ethan is horrified by the sight. He starts to go, but...

JEERING MAN (V.O.)
Take his wallet...you're out of a job now...

...Ethan reaches over to the Cabbie.

JEERING MAN (V.O., cont'd)
...and his gun.

EXT. RURAL ROAD - DAY
A little downscale poker bar. Outside, some OLD GUYS play
cards and drink booze.

Ethan jogs by in his captain's uniform. Blood soaks through
his dirty white pants.

EXT. RURAL ROAD - DAY
Ethan jogs. Sweat runs down his dirty face, cutting clean
troughs through the grime. His breathing is irregular, his pace
erratic. He kicks up dirt from the side of the road, trips and
regains his balance.

A PARALYTIC in a wheelchair crosses the road in front of
him, forcing Ethan to run around.

PARALYTIC
Ya tryin' ta kill me! Yeezus!

Ethan turns onto his street and trots up to the house. He rushes
inside, slams the door shut in our faces.

INT. BATHROOM - DAY
Ethan leans his face into the shower head as it sprays him with
steaming hot water. He grabs a towel and exits.

Ethan is ashamed. He leans into the mirror and is wracked by
sobs, then he rips the curtain rod from the shower and smashes

the mirror. He continues smashing the rod until it is a twisted tangle of partially shredded metal.

INT. ETHAN'S HOUSE, KITCHEN - DAY
Ethan is on the phone.

> ETHAN
> I'm sorry, Connie...no, that's it. I can't see you anymore, goodbye. That's right, I don't love you anymore. Just stay the hell away from me.

He hangs up.

> ETHAN (cont'd)
> Now are you happy? Well?

Ethan spins around, looking for the Jeering Man. He stalks through the house, opening doors, looking into rooms.

> ETHAN (cont'd)
> Hey! I'm talking to you, jerk-off! Are ya happy now? Are ya?

Ethan stands in a doorway expressionless, mute and drained. He's done.

> JEERING MAN (V.O.)
> Let's take out the motorcycle.

EXT. HIGHWAY - TWILIGHT
Ethan drives his motorcycle past a mist-enshrouded vineyard.

Bugs slam into his helmet. Inside the face plate, he stares straight ahead, like a zombie. His lips move as he talks softly to himself.

ETHAN

Why are you doing this to me?

The Jeering Man appears in front of Ethan's face, almost nose to nose, flying backwards in time with the motorcycle.

JEERING MAN

It's the only way. Scott must die. He got us fired. You hate him.

ETHAN

I can't let you do that. I won't.

Ethan brakes hard, screeching to a stop on the shoulder. He removes his helmet almost mournfully and drops it to the ground.

ETHAN

I don't care what you do to me, I ain't hurting Scott. He's my buddy.

JEERING MAN

He fired us. Don't you understand? Is he supposed to get away with it? Then what? Everyone will take advantage. Is that what you want?

ETHAN

No.

JEERING MAN

Then let's do it. Stop fighting me and things will be better.

ETHAN

I want things back the way they were.

                    JEERING MAN
Let's kill Scott.

                    ETHAN
I'll kill myself first. You wouldn't like that, would
you?

                    JEERING MAN
You're broken, you simply haven't realized it yet.
You need sleep. Why don't you sleep?

                    ETHAN
I don't wanna.

But he does. He's so tired he can barely stand up. His eyelids
flutter open and closed involuntarily. Ethan staggers into the
fence, tired to the bone and too dizzy to maintain his balance.

                    JEERING MAN
Sleep, Ethan.

Ethan sits by the fence. He tries to keep his eyes open, but it's
hard. His head leans back into a fence post.

A semi sprays loose gravel onto the shoulder. Ethan doesn't
flinch.

The Jeering Man flows into Ethan.

EXT. ETHAN'S HOUSE - NIGHT
The garage door is wide open, as is the door leading into the
house from the garage.

Connie's car pulls up to the curb and parks.

Connie gets out; she has been crying. She looks into the garage, puzzled.

                    CONNIE
     Ethan? Honey?

She walks into the house through the garage, noticing that it is
in disarray. The cat follows her.

INT. ETHAN'S HOUSE - NIGHT
Connie's feet step into frame with the cat directly behind.
Shards of glass on the carpet glint in the extreme foreground.
Connie looks down at the glass scattered outside and within
the bathroom, then sees the nearly empty frame where the
mirror once was.

Connie walks into the kitchen, sees the mayhem that has been
committed against the furniture and appliances. She cries
softly.

                    CONNIE
     Ethan?

The cat looks up at her and meows.

Flashing red and blue lights illuminate the living room.

EXT. ETHAN'S HOUSE - NIGHT
A police car parked in front of Connie's Honda so that she
can't leave. The lights on the rack go out and a POLICEMAN
gets out of the car.

Ethan's front door opens. Connie stands there with the cat in
her arms, bewildered and frightened.

INT. SHERIFF'S OFFICE - NIGHT
The cat walks across a well-ordered desk. An OFFICER on
the other side patiently observes as wet paw prints are left on
his papers.

                    OFFICER
      So you don't have any idea where your boy friend
      went to?

Connie takes the cat and sets him on the floor.

                    CONNIE
      I really should be going, I have to pick up my son at
      the sitters soon.

                    OFFICER
      You do realize why you're here?

                    CONNIE
      Ethan's in trouble?

                    OFFICER
      We're investigating the death of a cab driver. The
      driver that picked Mr. Russell up at Red Line just
      after he'd been fired.

                    CONNIE
      Oh.

                    OFFICER
      Tracks left at the scene lead straight to Russell's
      home. We'd like to know why.

Connie is stunned.

                    OFFICER (cont'd)
      Has he ever threatened you?

                    CONNIE
      I don't know what you mean.

The officer glances at a file on his computer.

OFFICER
I have a report here from a Nancy O'Connell, a nurse at Sonoma Memorial. She says he did threaten you.

CONNIE
But he didn't mean it. He was sick, that's why he was there.

OFFICER
Why don't you call your sitter and ask her to stay late, Ms. Wilcox?

EXT. FAIRMONT HOTEL, SAN FRANCISCO - NIGHT
A cable car creeps up one of San Francisco's steepest streets. PAN as it passes to reveal the ornate Fairmont Hotel.

INT. FAIRMONT HOTEL, LOBBY - NIGHT
The most beautiful lobby in San Francisco. Gold trim and magnificent carvings decorate the lavish interior. A lush red carpet muffles sound to a whisper, the furniture is elegant and chandeliers of light-filled cut crystal sparkle above.

Ethan purposefully strides into the lounge. Now he looks a little like the Jeering Man with a new haircut and his gait is similar too. Near the entrance, an easel with a sign advertising the current act, a jazz singer named "Eileen Barr."

INT. FAIRMONT HOTEL, LOUNGE - NIGHT
EILEEN smoothly delivers jazz tunes from the small stage. The dimly lit room is almost full.

Ethan sits by himself at a small table with a drink. A pretty woman (CANDY) squeezes through some patrons.

CANDY
Is this seat taken?

                    ETHAN
        Help yourself.

                    CANDY
        Thanks.

She sits.

                    CANDY (cont'd)
        What's your name?

                    ETHAN
        I don't know.

                    CANDY
        You're kidding.

Ethan frowns at her.

                    CANDY (cont'd)
        You aren't kidding?

                    ETHAN
        No.

She looks at his hand on the table. No rings.

                    CANDY
        Are you married?

                    ETHAN
        I don't know. I might be.

Ethan turns away to watch the singer. A drink arrives for
Candy.

                    CANDY
          My name is Candy.
                    (beat)
          I'm not married.

Ethan turns to her.

                    ETHAN
          You're better off.

INT. FAIRMONT HOTEL, HALLWAY - NIGHT
A door marked "512." A hand slips the electronic card key
into the reader and opens the door. Ethan and Candy walk in.
He flips on the lights. The room is gorgeous.

INT. FAIRMONT HOTEL, ROOM 512 - NIGHT
Candy lies on the bed in a pair of panties, picking at some
food in a room service tray while the TV burps out the local
news. There is a charge slip under a glass. She pulls it out.

Ethan brushes his teeth. Candy calls out to him from the main
room.

                    CANDY
          I thought you didn't know your name?

                    ETHAN
          Yeah?

                    CANDY
          Why does it say here "Doak Wilcox?" Who the hell
          is that?

Ethan pokes his head out.

                    ETHAN
          What did you say?

                              CANDY
            Doak Wilcox. That's what you signed on this bill...

                              ETHAN
                         (taking the bill)
            Give me that.

INSERT: The bill. It lists *ETHAN RUSSELL* as the card
holder, but the signature unmistakably reads *DOAK WILCOX*.

                              ETHAN
            This can't be...

                              CANDY
            What?

                              ETHAN
            It's right, but, why can't I remember?

                              CANDY
            Remember what?

                              ETHAN
            I don't know, I...

He stands before a large mirror, staring at his own eyes. They
morph to those of the Jeering Man. Ethan's face melts, giving
way completely to that of the Jeering Man.

                          JEERING MAN
            I am Doak. She is my wife!

                              CANDY
            You're married?

DOAK/ETHAN
I got sick and this is what happens! She took my son
and left me to die! Connie did this to me, betrayed
me! It's all her fault!

Candy is scared, she grabs at her clothes, hurriedly tries to get
into them.

Doak/Ethan pulls his belt out and wraps it around his fists.

ETHAN
She's just a tramp, like you.

EXT. ASTRAL PLANE
Astral Ethan rests in a fetal position, enshrouded by dark
swirling colors. The lights of his aura are dim. Around him,
the landscape is in constant flux.

DISSOLVE TO:

INT. INDOOR POOL - DAY
Ethan throws Shari high into the air. Shari splashes into the
pool. Sunlight drips in from huge, brilliant windows, setting
off crazy watery reflections everywhere. Shari surfaces, gig-
gling. A WOMAN at poolside smiles at them fondly. Shari
waves. The woman shakes her head.

SHARI'S MOM
Sorry, not today...

SHARI
Aw, Mommy, please?

But the woman shakes her head and that's that.

Ethan swims fast laps, cutting through the water like a shark.

103

Underwater. Brightly colored pool darts bounce lightly against the bottom. Shari grabs for as many darts as her small hands can hold. On her way back up to the surface, Shari sees something interesting. It's a below water tunnel cut through to the diving pool.

Shari surfaces and plops the darts down at pool's edge before diving right back in again. She swims for the tunnel with delight in her eyes. She's going to swim through to the other side and pop up in the other pool. Behind her, Ethan plows through the water.

Shari's Mom leafs through a magazine as Ethan swims. She looks over the paper's edge.

A couple of pool darts lay in a drying puddle on the far edge of the pool.

She goes back to her reading for a moment, but then looks over her paper again.

> SHARI'S MOM
>
> Shari?

Ethan keeps on swimming.

A huge clock on a timing board for university swim meets ticks the seconds away...

> SHARI'S MOM (cont'd)
> (urgently)
> Shari?

She gets out of her lounge hesitantly and walks around the pool, peering into it for any sign of her daughter.

SHARI'S MOM (cont'd)
Shari honey, let me know where you are, sweetheart.

Ethan swims to the edge fast, tucks into a turn and shoves back out into another lap.

Shari's Mom is concerned, she trots around the pool calling after Shari, but doesn't get a response. Seeing the adjacent diving pool, she makes a beeline for it. Someone dives in from above, sending wavelets and reflections scattering everywhere.

When it clears, a GOOD-LOOKING WOMAN SWIMMER surfaces. Behind her and below the water line, a grating.

SHARI'S MOM (cont'd)
Oh no...

SWIMMER
What's wrong?

Hair floats through the grating. Two little pinkish blobs rest on it, fingers, a child's fingers.

SHARI'S MOM
(shrieking)
Shari! Ethan! Oh my God!

Shari's Mother runs around the pool, following the grating with her eyes, trying to figure out where it opens up.

POV Ethan as he swims. Shari's Mom dashes in front of him, then jumps into the pool fully dressed.

Ethan stops, pulls his earplug out, wondering.

ETHAN
And she says she doesn't get PMS...

Shari's Mom surfaces, gasping, tugging at something below.
SHARI'S MOM (cont'd)
Get over here! Help me!

She grabs the side of the pool just as the Swimmer runs to her aid. Shari's Mom holds a foot to her chest and desperately tries to pull the body attached to it above water without letting go of the pool edge. The Swimmer jumps in to help.

ETHAN
Shit!

Ethan bolts through the water like a torpedo. He dives underwater and witnesses a tangle of legs and Shari's inverted body, her mouth gaping open, freely accepting water into her lungs. Ethan grabs her and pushes her torso and head out of the water.

The three of them pull Shari from the water. She is limp, lifeless. Ethan stares uncomprehending at his dead daughter. His wife turns on him with hatred burning in her eyes. She smacks him in the face with her fist.

SHARI'S MOM (cont'd)
You were watching her! You were supposed to be watching her! You!

She hammers his chest with her fists.

Ethan weeps.

DISSOLVE TO:

EXT. ASTRAL PLANE

Astral Ethan, still in a fetal position, now weeping as in the last scene, but then, ever so gently, a voice...

                    VOICE
        Children sleep very hard in life.

Astral Ethan slowly opens his eyes, as he does so, he becomes aware of his surroundings.

A huge star map on a wall. It is almost solid black, with pin-points of light scattered across it. There's something funny about the map though, no labels, and the dots of light grow rounded, three-dimensional, like real stars and planets.

Pull back to reveal a one room schoolhouse interior. Astral Ethan stands there with a GUIDE. The room has a blobby, overly physical quality to it, like it and everything inside is built out of Play-Doh.

                    GUIDE
        Look within yourself, you are not evil.

Astral Ethan does as he is told. Just like the star map, the colors of his aura are dark, but there are pinpoints of light everywhere.

                    ASTRAL ETHAN
        What is this?

                    GUIDE
        Virtue, your virtue.

                    ASTRAL ETHAN
        Are you trying to trick me?

107

The Guide reaches into Astral Ethan, carefully pulling loose what looks like a glowing silver thread.

> GUIDE
> You have already been deceived, but not by me. See this cord? You cannot relinquish your body until its time has come. You must go back.

Astral Ethan holds the cord in his hand, following it with his eyes. It seems to descend forever, disappearing miles beneath him.

> ASTRAL ETHAN
> Why? What for?

> GUIDE
> You cannot escape the price of your actions. The sooner you pay that debt, the greater your achievement will be.

> ASTRAL ETHAN
> What debt? I haven't done anything.

> GUIDE
> By your weakness, you have allowed your will to be dominated by another spirit. You share equally the responsibility for his actions.

> ASTRAL ETHAN
> And what am I supposed to do about it now?

> GUIDE
> End his domination. Drive his influence from you by your will to do good. Repair the damage you have done.

ASTRAL ETHAN

But...

The human form of the Guide is enveloped by his aura. It is powerful, bright, intense, beautiful. Astral Ethan cowers.

GUIDE
The debt will rise and your torment will be unendurable. Trust in my promise and not threats of evil.

Astral Ethan fingers the cord. He trembles in the light.

ASTRAL ETHAN
When will I see Shari again?

GUIDE
She is here.

Shari appears. She is faint, insubstantial.

SHARI
(firmly)
Don't let him hurt anyone else, Daddy. You have to go back. You can do it, I know you can.

Astral Ethan clearly can think of other things he'd rather do, but with Shari pleading with him, looking at him with her earnest eyes, it's hard to resist. He swallows hard before turning away.

A great dark tunnel opens before Astral Ethan, swallowing him whole. He tumbles into the darkness.

FADE TO BLACK:

FADE IN:

INT. FAIRMONT HOTEL, HALLWAY - DAY
Doak/Ethan strolls down the hallway. Ahead, two uniformed
POLICEMEN walk towards him led by a CLERK.
Doak/Ethan dips into a stairwell before they notice him. They
walk by the stair entry.

INT. FAIRMONT HOTEL, FIRE STAIRS - DAY
Doak/Ethan breathes evenly as he listens to the sound of
passing footsteps. After they fade to nothing, he quietly walks
down the steps as quickly as he can manage. When he reaches
the garage exit, he carefully opens the door a crack and peeks
out. His motorcycle is surrounded by POLICE, who busy
themselves examining it.

A POLICEMAN walks away from the door escorted by one of
the hotel STAFF.

                    POLICEMAN
          Did he make any calls?

                    STAFF
          Room service and the room itself, nothing else. All
          billed to his credit card.

They pass. Doak/Ethan slips out unnoticed.

INT. FAIRMONT HOTEL, LOBBY - DAY
POLICEMEN are stationed at every exit, and two others cir-
culate around the lobby. Ethan loiters out of sight, seething
with anger.

There is no way to exit without being seen. All the doors are
watched.

As Doak/Ethan's rage increases, black aural spikes appear all
around him. Like a bolt of lightning, they disperse suddenly
and violently.

A window explodes to his left, causing the police to run scurrying towards the source, leaving the main exit unguarded. Doak/Ethan walks quickly to the doors.

The desk clerk watches as Ethan passes; he is recognized.

                         CLERK
     Hey!

The huge glass doors swing shut. Doak/Ethan is gone.

The clerk runs out from behind his station, calling to the police.

                    CLERK (cont'd)
          I saw him! He just ran out the front! I saw the guy!

EXT. STREET, SAN FRANCISCO - DAY
Doak/Ethan rides a trolley up an incredibly steep street.

INT. FAIRMONT HOTEL, ROOM 512 - DAY
The door is laced with yellow crime scene tape. POLICEMEN range about the room bagging evidence. Candy's body lies in a body bag on the floor. The MEDICAL EXAMINER scrapes beneath her fingernails with a small tool and deposits the results in a baggie. Astral Ethan floats against the ceiling, invisible to everyone. He is horrified.

Below him, Candy's body. The Medical Examiner carefully returns her hand to the body bag. As he does so, her astral eyes open while her physical eyes remain closed. In similar fashion, her astral lips open as she speaks to Astral Ethan.

                         CANDY
          Connie's next, you need to stop him.

ASTRAL ETHAN

Are you hurt?

CANDY

You are still confused, you cannot see things as they are.

The M.E. zips the body bag shut

CANDY (O.S., cont'd)
Don't lose your focus, don't be like him.

INT. STATION-WAGON - DAY
A wiry little TOUGH OLD GUY drives. Doak/Ethan sits in the front passenger seat. Behind them, cages full of live chickens.

TOUGH OLD GUY
I'll tell ya this anyway, I ain't never havin' another cigar again. Never! Damn Clinton. The experience is completely wrecked now. You mind if I have a cigarette?

DOAK/ETHAN

Yes.

TOUGH OLD GUY
What? You don't wanna die of lung cancer like me? It's OK kid, I unnerstand.
          (cackles/chokes)
God, do I need a smoke.

DOAK/ETHAN
I just want to get home to my family. How much longer will it be?

112

> TOUGH OLD GUY
> To Sonoma? An hour, at least. You inna rush?

Doak/Ethan looks at his hands, at first they are blurry, then he sees two of each. He flexes them, trying to focus his eyes, but it gets worse. Doak/Ethan shuts his eyes for a moment.

EXT. ASTRAL PLANE
Astral Ethan floats before Doak/Ethan, watching.

INT. STATION-WAGON – DAY
Doak/Ethan opens his eyes, looks at the Tough Old Guy.

> TOUGH OLD GUY
> You got kids?

Doak/Ethan ignores him.

> TOUGH OLD GUY (cont'd)
> Well?

Doak/Ethan continues to ignore him.

> TOUGH OLD GUY (cont'd)
> Come on, fella, what, you want me to talk with my birds? Why do you think I gave you a ride?

> DOAK/ETHAN
> I have a son. His name is Matt...

> ASTRAL ETHAN (V.O.)
> Stay away from them.

> TOUGH OLD GUY
> How old is he?

113

                    DOAK/ETHAN
Five, ten. He's ten.

                    TOUGH OLD GUY
You don't know how old he is? What kind of father
are you?

                    ASTRAL ETHAN (V.O.)
A dead one.

                    DOAK/ETHAN
Go to hell.

                    TOUGH OLD GUY
Did I hear you right? You telling me to go to hell in
my own goddamn prince of a car? Well?

                    ASTRAL ETHAN (V.O.)
You gotta leave before you do anymore damage. I'm
takin' my body back.

                    DOAK/ETHAN
Or what? You pathetic weakling.

                    TOUGH OLD GUY
What? You punk!

Doak/Ethan's eyes glaze over.

                    TOUGH OLD GUY (cont'd)
That's it! I had enough of you!

Astral Ethan struggles, trying to get realigned with his body.
Astral Doak fights back, with Ethan's body the battleground.
It convulses as either combatant controls this or that limb,
then, Astral Ethan gets in all the way, but his hold is tenuous.

                    TOUGH OLD GUY (cont'd)
          Sonofabitchin' freak is what you are!

                          ETHAN
               (sleepy)
          Wait. Get the police, please, the police, get them...

                    TOUGH OLD GUY
          What are you saying to me now?

                          ETHAN
          Give them my name, Ethan Russell. Stop me before I
          do anything else. Dammit, this is so hard...

                    TOUGH OLD GUY
          What?

Ethan's body shakes with a severe internal struggle. His
countenance changes, becoming angry again.

                    DOAK/ETHAN (cont'd)
          No! Keep Driving! Keep driving or I'll kill you!

                    TOUGH OLD GUY
          You an' what army, mama's boy?

The car screeches to a stop.

                    TOUGH OLD GUY
          Get out.

The old man punches Ethan's door open, then kicks him out as
he guns the motor.

EXT. SIDE OF THE ROAD - DAY
Ethan tumbles out and the station-wagon drives away with one
door still open.

Ethan eats dirt. When he gets up, he radiates hatred.

POV; ETHAN. SIDE OF THE ROAD - DAY
The scene is considerably darker than before. Time lapse
storm clouds race across the sky, blackening it. Astral Ethan
appears, but he is faint.

> ASTRAL ETHAN
> (volume diminishes quickly to a low level)
> Let me in! Don't kill her! Listen to me!

> DOAK/ETHAN
> You don't exist anymore.

> ASTRAL ETHAN
> (faint)
> You'll only make things worse!

> DOAK/ETHAN
> Blithering weakling.

The scene darkens even more, obliterating Astral Ethan from
view. Dark malicious astral creatures move about this landscape turned nightmare as Doak/Ethan strides across it.

EXT. SIDE OF THE ROAD - DAY
Doak/Ethan walks along the shoulder of the road. Butterflies
and bees hover around some flowering plants.

EXT. POWER LINES - DAY
An ASTRAL HAND races along the cable. Astral Ethan zips
along at unimaginable speed, taking turns with gut-wrenching
swiftness. He releases the cable and continues, now even
faster.

He approaches a storefront with the speed of a meteor and plunges into it.

INT. HANKIN'S INSURANCE - DAY
Several OFFICE WORKERS go about their business. Connie stands near the fax, feeding papers into it.

Astral Ethan stands before her, shimmering.

> ASTRAL ETHAN
> Protect yourself, and Matt...

Connie gasps, brings her hand to her face in surprise. A SEC-RETARY stops near her.

Connie reaches out to him, tries to touch him. Astral Ethan vanishes.

> CONNIE
> Ethan? Ethan!

> SECRETARY
> Honey! What is it? Do you need to sit down?

> CONNIE
> I just saw Ethan. Right here, just a second ago.

Ethan is nowhere in sight, but the secretary glances around anyway.

> SECRETARY
> I would have seen him, honey. Maybe it was somebody else.

> CONNIE
> It was Ethan...

Then she realizes something, she may have seen a ghost.

> CONNIE (cont'd)
> ...he said I had to protect Matt...
> (nearly hysterical)
> I'm sorry, Gail, I have to go. Where's my purse?
> I need my keys. Where is it? Now, I have to go now.

Connie brushes past several people as she rushes to an office.

> CONNIE (cont'd)
> (hysterical)
> Excuse me, I have to leave...'need my keys, please,
> I have to hurry!

INT. CONNIE'S OFFICE - DAY
Connie cries as she looks around the office for her purse. She gets more and more frenzied the longer it takes to find it.

A WOMAN pokes her head in, Connie spins.

> WOMAN
> Is that what you're looking for?

She points.

INSERT: A chair in the corner. A purse hangs from the back.

EXT. PARKING LOT - DAY
Connie slams her door shut. The little Honda tears out of the lot.

INT. CAR, PARKING LOT - DAY
Two MEN sit in the front seat. A police flasher rests on the dash.

POLICE 1 (DRIVER)
Was that her?

POLICE 2
Bull's eye.

The driver turns the ignition, his partner picks up the radio.

POLICE 2
R 14 following subject West on Napa.

EXT. STREET, SONOMA - DAY
The unmarked police car zips through a red light.

INT. CONNIE'S APARTMENT, HALLWAY DAY
Connie trots down the hallway fingering her crucifix. Astral
Ethan is beside her, unnoticed.

CONNIE
(whispered)
Jesus protect my son from harm, shield him from the
work of the devil,...

ASTRAL ETHAN
Don't go in, Connie, get the police.

CONNIE
...in the name of Jesus, I rebuke thee Satan...

ASTRAL ETHAN
Downstairs, get the...shit! Connie!

When she gets to her door, she slides her key in the lock, turns
and shoves against it, but the door doesn't budge. The hotel
lock on the other side is engaged. Astral Ethan pushes through
to the other side.

<u>INT. CONNIE'S APARTMENT, HALLWAY - NIGHT</u>
Doak/Ethan stomps towards the door. Astral Ethan holds out his arms to stop him.

> ### DOAK/ETHAN
> It was so easy to take you and you think you can stop me now? Go back to Hell where you belong.

Doak/Ethan walks straight through Astral Ethan.

<u>EXT. CONNIE'S APARTMENT, HALLWAY - NIGHT</u>
Connie rings the doorbell repeatedly.

> ### CONNIE
> Matt! Open up, it's me!

Heavy footsteps approach from the other side of the door.

The latch clicks open.

Connie backs away from the door as it opens. Doak/Ethan stands in the doorway wearing scuffed and torn clothes. Behind him, Matt lies inert on the floor.

> ### CONNIE
> Matty!

Connie tries to push past Doak/Ethan, but he grabs her wrist and pulls her to him. His face fully morphs into that of Doak.

> ### DOAK
> No hello for your husband?

Connie screams. Doak shoves her into the apartment and slams the door shut. He clicks the hotel lock into place.

INT. CONNIE'S APARTMENT, DINING ROOM - NIGHT
Doak sits in the living room. Connie wipes Matt's face with a
wet towel. Astral Ethan watches helplessly.

                    MATT
          Mom? Ethan hit me.

                    CONNIE
          Sssh...

Doak spins to face her. Matt retracts in fear.

                    MATT
          Daddy?

                    DOAK
          I've been watching over you for the past five years,
          and the eight before that, protecting you, and this is
          what I get. Betrayal!

                    CONNIE
          I don't know who you are.

                    DOAK
          Yes you do! Don't deny it! You know my face, you
          know me! And you are my wife!

                    CONNIE
          Not anymore, I still have a life.

                    DOAK
          And you waste it on romance! I've been with you,
          I've advised you, but you never listen! Do you? Do
          you know how many men I've had to push away
          from you?

The glass coffee table spontaneously shatters.

121

DOAK (cont'd)
You should be thinking of me! Your husband! The
man you killed!

CONNIE
You killed yourself.

DOAK
(huge)
A LIE!

The television slams into a wall, imploding with a huge crash.

CONNIE
What have you done with Ethan?

DOAK
Ethan! Stupid little sailor boy! Stupid fantasies of
marriage! I'll kill you, you tramp!

Doak rushes over to Connie, but Astral Ethan rushes him at
the same time.

ASTRAL ETHAN
No!

He punches one of his arms into Doak, wriggling it into
alignment. Doak struggles against Astral Ethan, his face boil-
ing with rage. Spines of black astral light explode out of Doak,
piercing Astral Ethan, forcing him to withdraw.

ASTRAL ETHAN (cont'd)
Aaah!

Doak reaches for Connie and bludgeons her with his fist. Matt
flings himself over her just in time to catch a blow to his back.

Doak struggles with Matt, but the boy clings tenaciously to his mother.

>   MATT (cont'd)
>   I won't let you hurt her! Go away!

Astral Ethan gulps down air like a fish out of water as his aura fluctuates in and out from blacks to lighter colors.

Doak grabs Matt by the shoulders and heaves him across the room. Connie pushes Doak away and runs to Matt. Doak starts after her, but she throws a vase at him, scoring a direct hit on his face. She grabs Matt and rushes to the front door but Doak blocks it even as he pries bloodied glass from his cheeks.

>   DOAK
>   You don't go anywhere.

Matt scrambles out of her arms and runs to the bathroom. Connie races after him. Doak grabs at her dress as she flies over the threshold and Matt slams the door on Doak's fingers.

INT. CONNIE'S APARTMENT, BATHROOM - NIGHT
Matt is scared out of his mind.

>   MATT
>   Why does he want to kill us? Where did he come
>   from? I thought he was dead! What happened to
>   Ethan?

>   DOAK (O.S.)
>   You bitch!

The door shudders as if struck by a heavy object. Splinters and paint chips fall to the tiled floor.

Connie closes her eyes and prays.

The door is struck again, harder. But Connie doesn't flinch.

> CONNIE
> God protect us from evil and guide evildoers to the light of your wisdom. Protect my husband from sin as you protect us from him...

Connie's aura becomes faintly visible, then brighter.

> MATT
> Mom?

A ribbon of golden light sparks from her hands and trails out the door.

INT. CONNIE'S APARTMENT, LIVING ROOM - NIGHT
A golden ribbon of light flows into the room, probing it.

EXT. ASTRAL PLANE
Astral Ethan floats in blackness.

The ribbon of light appears dim in the distance, then grows brighter as it approaches Astral Ethan.

> CONNIE (O.S.)
> ...and bring back my Ethan to me that he might love as I love him...

The ribbon makes contact with Astral Ethan, rejuvenating him, making his aura brighten. As it does so, his background resolves into a more familiar pattern...

INT. CONNIE'S APARTMENT, HALLWAY - NIGHT
Doak heaves his body into the bathroom door.
He cracks it wide open, exposing Connie praying on the floor and Matt, scrambling out the window.

                    DOAK
    Now, you die.

Astral Ethan floats behind Doak, glowing brightly.

                ASTRAL ETHAN
    Not today.

Astral Ethan plunges into Doak.

                ASTRAL ETHAN (V.O., cont'd)
    I'm evicting you, now.

Doak tries to walk towards Connie, but it's like his legs are
encased in cement blocks. Connie backs away, but continues
to pray.

Doak flexes his fingers, straining against Astral Ethan's will.

                    DOAK
    I'm stronger than you, you can't stop me.

                ASTRAL ETHAN (V.O.)
    Try it on someone else, you don't scare me anymore.

                    DOAK
    My will is stronger. I am more confident. I will
    prevail. If not this way, then another.

Doak suddenly drops his hands and runs out of the room.

INT. CONNIE'S APARTMENT, KITCHEN - DAY
Doak rips open a drawer and rifles through its contents.

He slams the drawer shut.

A knife rack against the wall. Doak suddenly starts moving in slow motion. His hand reaches for the rack with all his muscular effort, but it's slow work.

DOAK
You want this too, I can feel it.

ASTRAL ETHAN (cont'd)
Forget about her, think of yourself!

DOAK
I'm thinking of you, now.

Doak's fingers close around a huge bread knife. With effort, he slides it across his left wrist.

DOAK
There! We both die then! Now neither one of us can have her!

ASTRAL ETHAN
There is so much more than you can see...

With difficulty, Doak switches the knife to his other hand. Connie feebly grabs his arm.

CONNIE
No! Ethan! Don't let him do it!

Doak slashes the other wrist. As the blood pours from his wrists, he changes, back to the body he's borrowed, back to Ethan. Astral Doak starts to separate from the body just as Astral Ethan becomes locked inside it.

ETHAN
Doak, look at yourself, remember who you were, see the good...

Darkness reaches in from the edges of the frame...

EXT. ASTRAL PLANE
A pinpoint of light. Another. The camera moves through a sparse constellation of pinpoint lights surrounded by fluid dark colors.

Pull back even more to reveal Doak, the lights sparkling inside his black aura. He falls through space as if from a great height, and then he connects, hard. He lies prone and hurting, barely able to breathe.

DISSOLVE TO:

INT. HYATT PLAZA - DAY
Tears smart from Connie's eyes. She bends down to cradle the broken form of a man on the floor. It's Doak, now lifeless.

A policeman stands nearby, holding a very small Matt in his arms.

Connie kisses Doak.

                    CONNIE
          Don't leave me, Doak, I need you...love you...don't
          go like this, please...

                    VOICE (V.O.)
          Do you remember this?

DISSOLVE TO:

EXT. ASTRAL PLANE
Doak is thunderstruck.

VOICE (V.O.)
She did love you, and others too.

A small knot of Astral figures approach Doak.

DOAK
Grandma? Paul?

A BEAUTIFUL OLDER WOMAN approaches Doak and embraces him. He clutches her for all he's worth, like a little boy in his mother's arms. The others surround him. They place their hands on him.

Very slowly, oh so softly, a tremendous pain-wracked cry wells up within Doak and his lights glow ever so slightly stronger, spreading, connecting, enlarging. The cry starts very small, barely audible, but increases in intensity as his astral body arches and stretches upward until the roar of his anguish is deafening.

The blackness snaps back into Doak's astral form. He is surrounded by a beautiful cool violet and blue light. He shrinks from it, fears it, submits to it. He crouches in the center of a vortex of blue flame, trembling.

VOICE (V.O.)
...you will learn from this...

Doak looks up. He is undeserving and knows it, his aura is tremulous with anticipation.

VOICE (V.O.)
...and be forgiven.

DOAK
(a whimper)
How?

FLASH TO WHITE:

INT. CONNIE'S APARTMENT, KITCHEN - DAY
Ethan stands in front of the sink. It is full of water and dishes mixed with blood.

ETHAN
What the hell?

He holds a bloody knife in his left hand. His left wrist bleeds from a deep slash. So does the right.

ETHAN (cont'd)
Goddamn, what...?

He looks around him, wondering how he got there. Woozy, he stumbles against the sink and falls. Ethan gets up and flips open a cabinet. He grabs some paper towels and tries to dress the wound, but he can't do it with one hand.

Ethan falls roughly to the ground, bangs his head against the sharp countertop as he goes down. Blood spills onto the lino-leum. The knife clatters to the floor.

Connie gathers him up in her arms.

Several POLICE OFFICERS crash through the front door.

MATT peeks from behind the shattered door frame as they spread out in the apartment.

One OFFICER approaches Connie.

OFFICER
Is this Ethan Russell?

129

CONNIE
Yes.

Connie cradles his head as blood leaks from his wrists onto the linoleum floor.

The Officer detaches his walkie-talkie.

OFFICER
R-13, we have the suspect. Let's get an ambulance out here guys, on the double. He's wounded.

DISSOLVE TO:

EXT. ASTRAL PLANE
A long, dark tunnel whooshes by on both sides in slow motion. Sounds of people talking, it's garbled, unintelligible.

VOICE
Connie Stephens, Wilcox? Connie Wilcox?...Yeah, she's the...right, eight six nine.

More voices, the tunnel wavers up ahead, a light, a figure in a bed, a shadowy figure. Two blurs, one in bed, the other sitting beside it.

INT. HOSPITAL, RECOVERY ROOM

CONNIE
Ethan? Can you hear me?

The blur in bed solidifies, it's Ethan. A fog that had obscured the view of Ethan and Connie disperses, the images sharpen, increase in contrast. Connie's voice becomes gritty, it's been sharpened also.

CONNIE (cont'd)
I took off from work early to see you, you know...

Ethan looks up at Connie. She has tears in her eyes. He tries to reach for her, but his arms are strapped to his sides. His movements are sluggish, drugged.

ETHAN
Wha-?

CONNIE
You had a concussion. They thought you might hurt yourself.

Ethan looks over his wounds as best he can.

ETHAN
Oh...

CONNIE
The doctor said you almost fractured your skull, banging it against the counter like you did.

ETHAN
Is Matt... OK? Was he hurt?

CONNIE
He's fine.

ETHAN
I didn't mean what I said before.

CONNIE
I know.

An ARMED GUARD stands just inside the door.

                    ETHAN
        This doesn't look like the same hospital...

                    CONNIE
        You're in prison, Ethan.

She's right. Ethan looks around himself, sees the signs everywhere.

                    CONNIE (cont'd)
        I'm sorry...

They hold hands. The auras around their hands glow and
merge and dance in a show of light.

                    DISSOLVE TO:

EXT. ASTRAL PLANE, THEATRE
The house is packed. Every person seen to date over the
course of the film and then some sit in the audience.

On screen in an over the shoulder uncut POV, Connie leaves
the prison hospital. In the audience, Astral Connie cries softly
to herself.

Astral Ethan stands near an USHER at the top of the aisle.

                    ASTRAL ETHAN
        Why would she accept this life?

                    USHER
        To help you. She has a strength you do not.

                    ASTRAL ETHAN
        What about me?

USHER

You have the opportunity to make up for past errors,
and learn a little more about the illusion you inhabit.

The screen, the audience and everything else but the Usher
and Ethan disappear.

ASTRAL ETHAN

It ain't gonna be easy.

USHER

In time it will be less difficult.

They sit, and as they do, the background changes. They sit on
solid hand-built wooden chairs resting on the porch of a house
built in the Alaskan wilderness.

ASTRAL ETHAN

I liked 1903...

USHER

...but you must move on.

ASTRAL ETHAN

Or get bored to death.

USHER (cont'd)

Have you decided?

ASTRAL ETHAN

It ain't so bad I guess... I get to do some things that
need to be done...

USHER

The life suits you well.

ASTRAL ETHAN
I always wanted to be a captain.

USHER
We are aware of that desire. Do you accept?

ASTRAL ETHAN
Yeah. Let's do it.

USHER
Ethan Russell...

As he says this, Ethan's face morphs to that of a BABY.

ZOOM IN on Baby's face, pull back, and it's in an old-fashioned crib sitting in a room decorated with circa 1940s furniture.

USHER (V.O., cont'd)
...be well.

Baby Ethan looks around, curious, as we

FADE OUT.

<u>THE END</u>

ABOUT THE AUTHOR

Andrew PAQUETTE has been working professionally as an artist in several different industries. He began his career as an editorial illustrator for such clients as *Time Magazine*, Bantam Books and CBS Records. Then, Andrew worked alternatively in comic books, where he co-created *Harsh Realm* (later a television series) with James D. Hudnall, video games and CG special effects. His credits include *Scooby-Doo*, *Space Jam*, *Daredevil*, *Full Spectrum Warrior* and *Spider-Man*. More recently, the versatile Paquette has been writing screenplays and exhibiting his watercolors and acrylics of the American Southwest (www.paqart.com) at the Taos Gallery in Scottsdale, Arizona.